JULIA

Dedication

Mitakuye Oyasin
All my relations

Munira

Illustrator's Dedication

With love and appreciation to:
Tom Eissinger whose persistence and devotion allow
us to learn and grow together;
my children, Adrien and Naomi, my most important teachers;
the memory of my mother, Ruth E. Neulicht,
whose unconditional love quietly nurtured me
and will continue to bless me forever.

JULIA

by
Munira Judith Avinger

Borealis Press Ltd.
Ottawa, Canada
2003

Canada

The Publishers acknowledge the financial assistance of the Government of Canada through the Book Publishing Industry Development Program (BPIDP) for our publishing activities

National Library of Canada Cataloguing in Publication Data

Avinger, Judith, 1941-
    Julia / Munira Judith Avinger.

ISBN 0-88887-271-2

I. Title.

PS8551.V56J84 2003   C813'.54   C2002-906125-3
PR9199.3.A9165J84 2003

Cover design by Bull's Eye Design, Ottawa
Illustrations by Lisa Neulicht
Photo credit – John Thompson
Typesetting by Chisholm Communications, Ottawa

Printed and bound in Canada on acid-free paper

Table of Contents

Illustrations

1.

The Tree

Julia looked at her mother angrily and said, "It's lunch time. I'm going outside."

"Fine," Mother said, "Go."

Julia opened the door to the cabin and then paused to grab an apple from the bowl on the counter. She slammed the door and ran down the path. She didn't stop running until she reached the old logging road. Then she stood for a moment and looked to her left and to her right, trying to decide which way to go. Finally she crossed the road and headed for a pine grove at the top of a small hill. As she climbed the hill, she saw a red squirrel race up a tree at the edge of the pine grove and perch on a branch. Julia was aware of him watching her as she entered the grove. She picked a tree opposite the squirrel's and bent down to feel the ground underneath. It was covered with pine needles and was fairly dry even though the cloudy sky threatened rain at any moment.

Julia sat down, leaning back against the tree, and began slowly eating her apple. She knew the squirrel was watching every bite she took. As she ate, she reviewed the argument with her mother. She had felt cross and tired all morning and she did not want to start learning algebra. She heard Mother's voice saying, "You've finished the math curriculum for the 8th grade and algebra is next."

"But I hate math. Couldn't I take a break and start it in the fall? After all, school's almost over for this year."

"No, you still have another month and there's no point in wasting time."

Julia closed her eyes and remembered the angry words that had followed. She felt two little tears trickle down her cheek. She thought about the day, two years ago, when her parents had told her they were thinking of leaving Montreal. They had seen an ad in the *Gazette* which said, "Family wanted to maintain large wooded property in the Eastern Townships. Non smokers, vegetarians preferred."

The property was owned by a rich doctor named Michel LaTendresse. Mother and Father never met the doctor himself. They talked only to his agent, who said they would be given a cabin in the forest to live in, plus a salary. Their job would be to maintain the road and the fences and watch for forest fires in the summer. Dr. LaTendresse wanted the property to be a refuge for wild animals so they would also have to enforce the No Hunting signs posted along the fence lines.

Julia had gone with her parents to see the property. There was a campground at the edge of the forest by a large clearing. The cabin they would live in was deep in the woods on a little hill surrounded by pine groves and large maple trees.

That night, back in Montreal, the whole family talked it over. Father said, "It's a beautiful property, and the salary is quite decent."

Mother said, "Yes, but we'd be so far back in the forest that it would be difficult for Julia to go to school. She'd have to study at home."

"Hurray!" Julia cried. She was eleven years old at the time and did not enjoy school.

Father laughed. "So you'd like to study at home, would you? You wouldn't give us any trouble?"

"No," Julia replied solemnly. "I'd do anything not to have to go to that school anymore."

So Father had called the agent, and it was settled. They moved at the end of the month. The first salary check arrived a few days later. Julia looked at the signature on the check— Michel LaTendresse, M.D. "I wonder if we'll ever meet the mysterious doctor," Mother said.

"I don't know," Father replied. "He seems to want to stay in the background."

Soon after they moved to the cabin, Julia's parents had spent several days walking in the woods with her, showing her the path to the creek and the logging road that led to the camp-ground. After that, they let her go out by herself as long as she didn't go too far from the cabin. Julia liked being alone in the woods. Sometimes she took a book and spent hours just sitting in the pine grove, reading and watching the squirrels and the birds and listening to the mice scurry through the dead leaves in the autumn as they started looking for their winter nests. She also liked to watch the butterflies. Some were pale yellow and others had orange wings with white spots. And she liked the blue dragonflies down by the creek and the caterpillars who curled up in fuzzy little balls when they were startled. She didn't like the flies and mosquitoes, however. They made sitting in the woods difficult in the summer.

As Julia grew more familiar with the woods, she was allowed to go farther from the cabin. Sometimes she surprised a deer, who would bound away, leaping gracefully over bushes and fallen trees, white tail held high. In the winter, she would find the deer's nests in the pine groves. They hollowed out beds for themselves in the snow and Julia could see their tracks and their droppings under the pine trees. She wished the deer wouldn't run away from her, but she knew that they were often hunted, both by humans and by other animals, and it was their nature to be cautious. Sometimes at night she could hear the coyotes howling and she would shiver, thinking of the deer and wondering how they felt when they heard that eerie wailing.

Julia sighed and ate the last bite of her apple. She looked at the core and then tossed it across the pine grove, underneath the tree where the squirrel was waiting. She watched as he ran down the tree and picked up the apple core between his front feet. He took quick little bites, looking nervously at Julia as he ate. She sat still until he finished and then she stood up.

She sighed again and said out loud, "Why do I feel so frustrated? What do I want?" She walked back to the logging road. There were many sugar maples in this part of the woods. They were especially thick throughout a large circular area which surrounded an old sugar cabin. Julia walked through the maple grove until she came to a particular tree.

She stood on the road, thinking about the first time she'd noticed this tree. It was in late October, a few months after she'd moved to the woods. She had been walking down the logging road when she saw it—an old maple, not far from the road, with a wide gnarled trunk and long curving branches, two of which were reaching out toward her like beckoning arms. She had stopped abruptly and looked up at those branches. The leaves were half green and half orange, their colours soft in the cloudy air.

As she watched, the wind had blown lightly and a few leaves had let go, falling gently to the earth, one of them landing on Julia's head. She had taken off her glove and pulled the leaf from her hair. Then she looked at it carefully. It was a dull orange colour and had holes in it where insects had chewed. She put it in her pocket. When she got back to the cabin, she took it out and placed it in a little box on top of her dresser. The next morning it had curled up and turned brown, but Julia didn't throw it away. In the days that followed, she looked at the leaf often, studying it as if she were waiting for it to tell her something.

Every time Julia walked down the road that autumn, she was aware of the old maple. When the snow came in December, she glided by on her skis, hurrying past the tree, whose branches now held rounded piles of snow. One day some of this snow slid off a branch just as Julia was passing and landed on her head. She stopped and looked up at the tree. Then she skied around to the other side. She saw a deep hole in the trunk where a branch had fallen off. Inside the hole, she saw the droppings of a porcupine, who had once found shelter there. She stood beneath the tree for several minutes, looking up at the tall, wide trunk. She could see the bare spots where the porcupine had chewed the bark. The tree looked old and somehow wise. Julia spoke out loud, "You remind me of my grandfather. He used to tell me stories." She paused and then said, "But he's dead now."

With the coming of spring, Julia began spending more time near the tree. She watched as the buds began to open and the pale-gold maple blossoms formed, followed by the opening of the first tiny leaves. By the end of May, the leaves were full and deep green. One day in mid June, when the sun was hot, Julia came to the tree looking for a shady place to sit and read. The ground under the wide branches was soft with a cushion of dead leaves and ferns.

She sat down and leaned back against the trunk and opened her book. She read a few pages and then started feeling sleepy from the warm air. She closed her eyes and let the book slip from her lap. Her mind drifted into a vague dream about huge green leaves blowing in a gentle breeze. She was lying on one of these leaves like a baby in a cradle, rocking back and forth in the sunlight. Back and forth, back and forth—the shadows of the leaves above her slid across her face. It was so peaceful. She started to slip into a deeper sleep when suddenly, she heard a voice whispering close in her ear—"It's time to wake up now."

Julia sat up with a start, her heart beating wildly. She looked around at the forest. "Who said that?"

There was no answer and she started to relax. "It must have been part of the dream," she told herself.

She leaned against the tree and closed her eyes, but before she could go back to sleep, she heard the voice again. "No, it wasn't a dream."

She opened her eyes, but again no one was there. "Who are you?" She spoke out loud.

"Relax. You don't have to shout. In fact, you don't have to speak at all. I'm right here. You're leaning against me."

"The tree?" Julia sat up again and looked around at the trunk of the old maple.

"You could say I'm a tree. Lean back again and relax so we can talk. You don't have to speak out loud. Just send me your thoughts. I'll hear them."

Julia leaned back again, thinking, "I must be crazy. I'm talking to a tree."

"No, you aren't crazy. Anyone who spends enough quiet time alone in the woods will start talking to trees."

"Maybe, but they don't generally talk back."

"Of course they do. You just have to listen carefully."

Julia considered this for a moment and then said, "I think you've been trying to get my attention for a long time. You dropped a leaf on my head—and some snow, too."

"Yes, that's true. I could see you were ready."

"Ready for what?"

"For instruction."

"But I'm getting lots of instruction already—history, science, French, and math." Julia made a face as she thought about math.

"This is a different kind of instruction."

"What kind?"

"You'll see as we go along."

"Is this a mystery?"

"If you want it to be."

Julia waited to see if the tree would say anything else. Slowly she picked up her book and started to stand up and then she heard the whispering words again. "And you can throw away the dead leaf now. You don't need it anymore."

Julia looked at the tree in astonishment. "How did you know about the dead leaf?"

She waited again, but there was no answer. She walked back to the cabin, lost in her thoughts. When she saw her parents were out in back working in the garden, she was glad. She didn't want to talk to anyone. She went quickly to her room and picked up the box which held the leaf. It was so dry it was beginning to crumble. She took the box outside and dumped the leaf on the ground. She watched it settle into the mass of leaves and sticks on the floor of the forest. She had the brief impression that it was glad to be back outside. She shook her head and walked inside. She sat down in the rocking chair by the kitchen window and looked out at the sunlight. She thought about the conversation with the tree and said, "Maybe it was just my imagination," but somehow she knew it wasn't. "Well," she told herself, "I may be crazy and I certainly can't tell anyone about this, but it's definitely going to be interesting."

After that Julia had gone to the tree often. Whenever she felt angry or sad, she had sat under the shelter of his leaves in the summer or stood in the snow with her arms around his trunk in the winter. She had told him her problems and waited for his answer. When it came, it was often both comforting and challenging, like her grandfather's stories, which always had a moral at the end.

And now, Julia was standing under the tree again, telling him about the fight with her mother. She laid her hand against his trunk and said angrily, "It's not fair. Why do I have to go to school with my parents? They don't understand me. I want to go back to regular school."

She waited for his response, but all she heard was the wind and a yellow-bellied sapsucker tapping on the roof of the old sugar cabin on the other side of the logging road.

"OK," she said finally. "I know. I have to make my mind quiet or you won't talk to me."

She sighed and sat down on the ground beneath the tree. She leaned back and closed her eyes and listened to the banging of the sapsucker for a while and then slowly the words of the tree began to form in her mind. "You chose this life."

"I did not." Julia sat up straight and opened her eyes. She looked up at the branch above her head. "I'm just a kid. Nobody even asked me if I wanted to come here."

"Nevertheless, you made your choice. You just don't remember. Besides, you didn't like school. You were shy, afraid to talk in class. You couldn't wait to get home in the afternoon."

Julia didn't like this response. She wanted sympathy, but she felt too tired to argue anymore. She leaned back against the tree and said, "So what am I supposed to do?"

"Nothing. Just relax for a while."

Julia closed her eyes again and let her mind drift until it came to a focus at the place where her back met the hardness of the tree trunk. She could feel the rough bark through her shirt. It was slightly uncomfortable, but she was too tired to move. She felt herself settling down deeper into the ground beneath the tree. Gradually, the roughness of the bark began to fade as though the cells of the tree and the cells of her body were dissolving and merging together like the molecules of gases in the diagrams in her science book.

Julia realized that she could no longer feel her body at all. Her mind was moving slowly into the awareness of the tree.

She felt the sensation of being rooted in the earth, the solid stillness of the heart wood at the center of the trunk, the faint stirring in the sap wood as the warmth of the sun penetrated the bark. She felt the slight pressure of a bird landing on a branch and the trembling of the leaves as a breeze passed.

She was aware of memories, too—memories of the letting go of the leaves in the autumn and the long sleep of winter under a blanket of snow—memories of the scraping teeth of the porcupine and the bending of a high branch under his weight as he sat looking out at the forest after his meal.

It was restful to be a tree. There was nowhere to go and not much to do—just accept the changes in the weather, the awakening of spring, when the consciousness moved upward with the sap to the opening blossoms and the tiny new leaves, which drank the rain as it fell.

The rain—Julia sat up and opened her eyes as a rain drop landed on her forehead. She shook herself and looked at her hands, half expecting to see branches and green leaves, but her fingers were still there. She turned around and looked at the tree. "Was I once a tree—like you?" she asked softly.

The answer came quickly. "Well, you could say that you are a tree now—and a bird and a deer and a rabbit and a mosquito ..."

"No, not a mosquito," Julia interrupted.

"Yes, a mosquito and a porcupine and a mouse and other people, too. It's all happening at the same time. In fact, there's really no place where your mind stops and other minds start."

"Is this what they're learning in the real school?" Julia thought suddenly that maybe she'd been missing something.

"No, this isn't what they're learning. This is something that doesn't have to be learned. It only has to be remembered. Unfortunately, few people do remember."

"Then why did I remember? Am I special?"

"No, you aren't special. You just stopped talking and thinking long enough to listen for a while."

Julia waited for a few minutes, but the tree didn't speak again so she stood up. The rain was falling gently and she realized she was getting wet. She walked down the road to the

cabin, thinking about what it had felt like to be inside the mind of the tree. When she reached the cabin, she found her mother cleaning the kitchen. Julia realized that her anger had completely disappeared and she wanted to talk. She didn't know how to describe her experience with the tree, however. She just said, "Mother, do you remember being a tree?"

Mother gave her a strange look. "A tree? What are you talking about?"

Julia shrugged her shoulders. "Nothing. I think I'll go back out for a few minutes and then I'll come inside and we can start the algebra."

"But it's raining."

"Not hard. In fact, it's letting up."

Mother paused for a moment, still looking at Julia, and finally said, "OK, that's fine."

Julia put on a dry shirt and went back outside. Once again she walked up to the pine grove. She stood under the trees and closed her eyes. She could feel the minds of all the creatures around her. She could feel a bird flying overhead, singing for joy. She could feel a little mouse hiding under the leaves on the ground and the tall pine trees giving their fragrance to all the creatures of the forest. She smiled as she realized that she could even feel one of the first mosquitoes of the season, hovering behind her head, looking for a spot of bare skin. Julia felt happy. She knew that what the tree had said was true, although she found she couldn't think about it too much with her brain without getting confused. She opened her eyes and looked up at the branches of the pine trees against the cloudy sky. She knew that the old maple tree had helped her remember something important. She also knew that more lessons lay ahead, which made her feel both excited and a little bit nervous.

2.

Bugs And Birds

The morning after her experience with the tree, Julia woke up early. She lay in bed thinking, "What day is it?" She reviewed the week, counting each of the chapters she'd read in her French book. Five—five chapters, five days. "It's Saturday." She sat up with a smile. "No lessons today." She got up and looked out her bedroom window. The sun was shining through the tops of the trees. "Saturday and sunshine—perfect."

Julia dressed and went out to the kitchen. Her parents were already at the table.

"You look happy today," Father said.

"It's Saturday—and it's sunny."

"A good day to roam the woods?" Mother asked.

"Yes."

"Well, we do need some help in the garden—perhaps in the afternoon. Then you could have the morning free."

"OK," Julia said. "I'll help you right after lunch."

She hurried through the breakfast dishes, which was one of her daily chores, and then put on her shoes and ran outside. As she closed the cabin door behind her, she felt a rush of freedom. She continued running down the path to the logging road and then stopped. Where should she go? She considered the pine grove across the road. The sun was brushing the tops of the trees and sending rays of light down into the interior of the grove. It was beautiful and inviting, but Julia shook her head. "No," she said, "today I want water." She turned and headed down the road toward the creek.

When she reached the old maple tree, she paused. "Should I go talk to him?" She thought about her experience of the day before and then said, "No, I said no lessons today and that includes him." She continued down the road.

When she reached the creek, she took off her shoes and sat down on the little bridge. She dangled her feet into the cold

11

water. She could see tiny fish swimming around under the bridge. Sometimes one would brush lightly against her toes. She also saw the insects that skimmed over the surface of the water. She had studied these insects in her science class with Father. She'd learned that they fed on other insects which floated on the surface of the creek and that their proper name was water strider. Julia called them waterbugs. She liked to watch them. When they came into the sunlight, they were followed by delicate cross-shaped shadows, which darted back and forth behind them.

Julia liked the way they moved, with a sudden swift sideways jump, followed by a moment of total stillness. Sometimes the paths of two insects would cross and there was an instant of acknowledgment when their antennas almost met and then the sudden leap when each one moved quickly back into its own space as though it had touched something hot. It reminded Julia of an experiment she'd done a few months ago. Father had brought two magnetic rods from town and he told Julia to first touch the positive end of one to the negative end of the other. She did and the magnets flung themselves together like long lost friends. Then Father said, "Now try the two negative poles."

Julia turned one of the rods around in her hand and held its negative end up to the other one. She found it was impossible to bring the two negative poles together. The magnets jumped away from each other just like the waterbugs except that with the bugs, there was that one tiny instant of recognition.

Julia was intrigued. She hopped down from the bridge into the shallow water. She knelt in the sunlight and waited for the waterbugs to recover from the shock of her arrival. It wasn't long before they started darting back and forth again. She picked one insect and focused all of her attention on it. Slowly she felt her mind begin to jump over the surface of the water. After each jump, there was the pause, the moment of gathering force and then the next quick sideways leap. She continued to follow with her mind until, suddenly, there it was—another waterbug—the two were almost touching. It happened so fast she almost missed it—a spark between the antennas of the two insects— and then the quick jump away from any further contact.

Julia stood up, realizing that her shorts were soaking wet. The waterbugs puzzled her. Why were they repelled by their own kind? How did they manage to mate if they couldn't make contact? She walked slowly back up the road, wondering about what the tree had told her. He had said that she was part of all creatures, which must include waterbugs. It's true that she had been able to penetrate their consciousness, but what she'd found seemed strange, even alien. As she walked by the tree, she said, "I'll have to ask you about that some time—but not yet," and she hurried past him on her way back to the cabin.

School was over the end of May and, except for her chores, Julia was free to wander through the woods as she pleased. Most days she took a book with her, but often she forgot to read it. She was in a dreamy mood, happy to sit for hours, letting her mind roam from one creature to another, practising what she'd learned from the tree. Briefly she would think about going back to him to ask about the waterbugs, but she kept saying, "Not yet, not yet." She knew he was waiting for her—that there was more he wanted to tell her—but she wasn't ready to listen. She felt as though she were drifting through a happy dream. She was afraid the next lesson was going to make her wake up—and she didn't want to wake up, at least not yet.

One day in early June, Julia walked down to a clearing close to the campground on the edge of the forest. There were wildflowers growing everywhere and mourning doves sitting on the power line that carried electricity to the camp. She loved to listen to the mourning doves. They reminded her of the flute her father played sometimes in the evening while her mother strummed softly on her guitar. Father's music was always slow and peaceful. When she listened to him play, her thoughts became smooth like the music and, if she closed her eyes, she could see a stream of light that flowed through her mind like the water in the creek. Sitting there in the meadow, among the wildflowers, she closed her eyes again, and listened to the call of the doves.

When she opened her eyes, she saw two butterflies fluttering around the flowers in the clearing. They seemed to be playing with each other. Their pale yellow wings often touched as they dipped down into the center of a blossom. Julia leaned closer to watch them. She could feel the lightness of their flight through the still summer air. She knew it was almost lunchtime, but she didn't want to leave the butterflies. She closed her eyes again and let her mind drift along with them from flower to flower and slowly she began to realize that the butterflies weren't just flying together. They were also communicating with each other. Brief wordless messages were flowing from one to the other in an almost constant stream of energy. Julia could feel their signals, but she couldn't quite understand them.

Abruptly, she opened her eyes as a sudden wave of sadness came over her. The feeling was so strong it brought tears to her eyes. Her heart beat fast for a moment, the way it did when she was awakened suddenly from a dream. She wanted something and she knew what it was—she wanted someone, not a tree or a squirrel, or a butterfly, but another person, a friend, someone she could talk to, who would understand her thoughts and her feelings.

She considered her parents. They were nice people and she knew they loved her. Maybe she could talk to them. Then she shook her head as she remembered the look in her mother's eyes the day she'd asked her if she remembered being a tree. No, her parents wouldn't understand, and anyway, they were busy right now. The weather had been hot and dry for June and it was a dangerous time for forest fires. Every day Father would drive down to the campground to talk to the manager there and make sure everything was all right. Several times a day Mother would climb up the steps of the fire-watching tower behind the cabin and gaze out into the treetops with binoculars, searching for any signs of smoke. Julia stood up and started back to the cabin, suddenly feeling very much alone.

When she woke up the next morning, Julia lay in bed listening to the birds. They were all singing together like a choir gone wild. Julia liked to see if she could separate the various songs as she listened so she could hear them more clearly. Suddenly, in the midst of all the cheeping and warbling, she heard the faint flute-like call of a mourning dove. She was excited. Normally, she couldn't hear the doves from the cabin because they didn't come into the deep forest. She listened as the same two notes sang out over and over. "The wind must be blowing from the clearing," she told herself. "It's carrying the song to me."

As she listened intently to the mourning dove, the songs of the other birds began to fade into the background. Her eyes were still closed and she began to see the same stream of light she saw when her father played the flute. She felt her mind let go and start to follow that light, which seemed to be carrying her closer to the song of the dove.

The two notes were growing stronger and the chorus of birds around the cabin receded even farther into the background. The call of the dove became louder and louder until it seemed to be coming from right behind Julia's head. She opened her eyes. Instead of her bedroom, she saw a thick dark branch and a canopy of green leaves. Through the leaves, she could see the sky glowing with the sunrise. Underneath her body she could feel three warm, round eggs. She was sitting in a nest. She looked around and saw a bird perched on a branch just above her. She watched as he patiently sang his only song over and over. She knew that this bird was her mate and that the eggs she was sitting on were full of life, kept warm by the heat of her own body. She also knew that soon her mate would come to take her place and she would fly off in search of seeds.

When the sun was up, her mate flew down to the nest and she hopped onto the branch. She spread her wings and rose into the air. She flew straight and steady, riding the current of air she made with her beating wings. She could see the campground down below. No one was stirring yet. She knew there was a field just beyond the row of trees behind the tents where she could gather a supply of seeds. She saw other birds flying here and there, busy now that the morning concert was over.

When she reached the field, she quickly flew down to the tall meadow grass and gathered the seeds in her beak. Then she flew back up into the air toward the trees that lined the campground. As she cleared the trees, she looked down at the

tents—blue and green and orange—and she was vaguely aware
of the dreams of the sleeping campers. She flew to the nest and
her mate left to find his own seeds. The sun rose steadily in the
sky and the two birds took turns sitting on the eggs and gathering seeds. Sometimes, they would stop and rest on the power
line and the male bird would sing again. The afternoon came
and went and the sun dipped low in the west. The evening chorus began and the male dove joined in, singing the same two
notes over and over. When the sun disappeared and darkness
came, all the birds became silent. They tucked their heads into
the feathers on their breasts and they slept.

In the morning, they woke with the first light and the same
routine began again. The male dove sang steadily while the
female sat on the nest. When the first rays of the sun appeared,
he came to the nest and she flew off to gather seeds. Again she
flew over the campground, looking down at the tents. On her
way back to the nest, she flew down lower where she could see
the outlines of the tents more clearly. Then suddenly, she saw
something else—a reddish glow which was slowly spreading
from a dead branch that lay on the ground a few feet from one
of the tents. A little breeze stirred the still air and a trail of
smoke began to rise from the glowing branch. The bird flew to
her tree, but she didn't land. Something was tugging at the back
of her mind. She flew back over the campground again, circling
that little spot of red and the smoke which was growing thick-
er. She returned to it three times, pulled there by a message
from deep inside her mind—and then suddenly, with a start,
she remembered.

Julia opened her eyes and sat up quickly in her bed. "Fire,"
she gasped in a choked voice, and then, realizing that no one
could hear her, she screamed, "Fire! Fire!" Julia's parents came
rushing into her room.

"Fire—where?" Mother said, looking anxiously around the
room.

"At the campground."

"The campground?" Father said, "How do you know?"

"I just know" Julia answered, "Please, Father, please go
quick."

Mother looked hard at Julia and then said quietly, "You'd better go, Jack."

"All right," he said. He went back to his room and dressed quickly. Then he went out and drove down the logging road in the old jeep. Julia got up. She went to the kitchen and sat down to breakfast with her mother. Neither one of them spoke. They tried to eat, but they weren't really hungry. They both kept looking out the window, waiting for Father to return.

Finally, they saw the jeep drive up. Father got out and walked slowly up to the house. He came through the door and sat down at the breakfast table. Mother said, "Well?"

"There was a fire all right. One of the campers didn't douse his campfire last night and there were still coals this morning. There were some dead branches he'd been using for kindling lying on the ground beside the fire pit. All it took was a little breeze to blow a spark in the direction of those branches. Everything's so dry right now, it didn't take long for it to catch. Fortunately, one of the campers woke up and found it before it had a chance to spread and he had it out by the time I got there."

Father paused and then he looked at Julia, who remained silent. "Julia," he said. "How did you know?"

"I just knew."

"Did you dream it?" Mother asked.

"Yes, that's it—it was kind of like a dream." Julia didn't dare tell them about being the bird. She knew that sometimes people had dreams that told the future. She'd read about these dreams in one of her books.

"Well," Father said. "Well, I just don't know, that's all. I didn't know what to tell the campers when I came rushing in so early in the morning. They were so excited about the fire, though, that they forgot to ask me why I was there."

He looked at Julia and said, "Well," again and then got up and went and stood by the window, gazing out at the trees.

Julia looked down at her cereal bowl, staring at two blueberries that were floating on top of the milk. She knew her mother was still watching her. Finally, Mother said, "I guess we'd better get moving. We have a lot to do today." Julia

breathed a sigh of relief. She wouldn't have to explain anything—yet—but once again she had the feeling that she needed someone she could talk to.

When Julia left the cabin that morning, she went straight to the
tree. She sat down underneath his broad branches and said
silently, "I'm back."

She waited a few minutes and finally he began to talk to
her. "I see that you're back."

"I need someone to talk to."

"Yes, I see that, too. But why are you so anxious? Don't you
know that everything you need will come to you in time?"

"Will it?"

"Yes. Right now you're afraid of what you know so you're
afraid to share it. You will find out later that you don't really have
anything until you learn to share it. Now, go back home and stop
worrying. Nothing can happen as long as you're worrying."

"But I wanted to ask you something—about the waterbugs."

"Yes?"

"Why did they seem so strange? You said I'm part of every
creature that exists, but I don't feel like part of the waterbugs."

"Many things will seem strange to you—even the minds of
other people."

"But the waterbugs?"

"The waterbugs have found a way to co-exist. They won't
have enough to eat if they waste their time fighting over terri-
tory so they cooperate by getting out of each other's way. Some
humans could learn from that."

"I see. I was afraid to come talk to you because I didn't
want the next lesson, but it isn't so bad after all."

"No, it's like the algebra."

"The algebra?" Then Julia remembered the fight with her
mother about learning algebra. "That's true. Algebra wasn't so
bad once I got started."

Julia got up and slowly began to walk back to the cabin.
She was feeling better. The tree had only told her what she
already knew. She needed to talk to someone about what she

was learning from the tree, but she was afraid. She was afraid people wouldn't understand. But he said everything she needed would be provided so all she had to do was relax and wait. She stopped for a moment. She looked up at the sun shining through the leaves and thought, "Well, the sun keeps shining and the birds keep singing. The tree said everything will come in time so I guess I'll just have to practise being patient."

3.

Squirrels

Julia resumed her regular visits to the tree. One hot day in July, she sat in the shade under his branches and said, "There's something that bothers me. With the waterbugs and the butterflies, I could see through their minds, but I still knew I was Julia. But with the dove, I forgot completely. It seemed to go on for such a long time—one whole day and night. It was only when I saw the fire that I remembered. That scared me. What if I forget I'm a girl? I like the mourning doves, but I don't want to be one."

The tree didn't answer immediately and Julia had the feeling he was considering his words carefully. Finally, he said, "Do you know what trust means?"

"Trust? Yes, it means having confidence in something."

"Do you have confidence in yourself?"

"In myself? I don't know. You mean if I have confidence in myself, I won't forget I'm a girl, not a bird?"

"No, it means you won't forget who you really are—which is neither a bird nor a girl."

"That doesn't make sense. I am a girl." Julia opened her eyes and looked down at her body, dressed in blue shorts and a yellow shirt. "I am a girl," she repeated.

"You're playing the role of a girl, but who you really are is far beyond that body you're looking at."

Julia closed her eyes again and considered what the tree had said. Finally, she asked, "And who am I really?"

"Yes, that's the question you should be asking. But I can't tell you the answer. It has to come from the inside. And it will if you aren't afraid."

"So, all I have to do is relax and not worry, right? That's what you keep saying."

"Yes, I keep saying that so why haven't you learned it yet?"

21

Julia thought about this question throughout the hot summer days while she was being patient, waiting for the friend the tree had said would come to her. In August she had to help her parents as they started harvesting the garden. She sat in the shade snapping green beans or cutting tomatoes for the canning jars and asked herself, "Why don't I know who I really am? It must be a secret. Maybe I'm really a princess in exile and these kind people have adopted me." She looked at her mother kneeling between the carrots rows. "It's true I do look like her, but maybe that's why she was chosen. Maybe my true family has all been wiped out by evil terrorists and I'm the only one left."

Julia looked down at the tomato she was about to cut. It was bright red and full of life. She started to picture what it was like to be a tomato, but quickly pulled her mind back. "I won't be able to cut them if I know how they feel," she told herself.

Then she looked at her hands wet with tomato juice and her knees covered with dirt. She didn't feel much like royalty. "But, of course, that could be part of the disguise." She considered again the possibility that she was a princess.

Julia sighed and her mother looked up from the carrots. "Are you ready for a break?" she asked.

Julia put down her knife. "A break would be nice. I'm thirsty." She went into the kitchen and poured herself a glass of water. She sat down on the rocker and said softly, "The tree says it has to come from the inside. This must be the really big lesson."

As autumn came and school started again, Julia was still puzzling over the question the tree had asked. One afternoon, after she finished her lessons, she sat down on the ground beside a birch tree and tried to catch the yellow leaves as they fell from the branches. As she sat there, she saw a squirrel run through the dead leaves on the ground and up the trunk of a tree. The squirrel was obviously busy and Julia thought, "He's probably getting ready for the winter."

That night the wind turned cold and Mother made a fire in the wood stove. After Julia went to bed, she lay there for a while listening to the fire crackle and the wind blow. Her eyes

closed and she was just about to drift into sleep when suddenly she heard another sound above the wind and the fire—a
thumping, rustling sound and then the scamper of little feet,
running through the insulation in the ceiling just over her
head. Julia sat up and called her parents, "Mother, Father, come
here. There's an animal in the ceiling."

Julia's parents came quickly into her room. They sat down
on the bed beside Julia and listened. There were a few seconds
of silence and then it came again—the pattering of little feet
just over their heads.

"It's a squirrel," Father said. "He must have found an opening in the wire mesh we put around the eaves. We'll have to
check it tomorrow. There isn't much we can do tonight."

So that night Julia had to sleep with the sound of the squirrel running back and forth over her head. The next morning
she watched as Father climbed up the ladder and found the
hole in the wire. He came back down, shaking his head, saying,
"The guy in the hardware store told me that squirrels couldn't
chew through this wire, but there's a hole the size of a ping-
pong ball up there and it didn't just appear by itself."

Julia climbed up the ladder to examine the hole. As she
looked at it, she could see in her mind the image of the squirrel bending down from the overhang of the roof, chewing that
little hole with his sharp front teeth.

Father said, "Well, I guess I'll have to make another trip to
the hardware store and get some tougher wire."

Mother said, "Let's make sure the squirrel is out before we
put the wire up."

"Maybe we can catch him. Then we'll know for sure he's
out."

Father left right after lunch and came back late that afternoon. In the jeep he had a roll of strong wire mesh. He also had
a large cage with a little tray in the middle and a door on each
end with wires that fell down over the openings and barred
them shut. It was the movement of the tray that made the
doors fall. Julia watched as her parents wired a piece of apple to
the tray and set the lever that held the doors open. They lined
the trap with newspaper and hung it from the eaves of the

cabin so it rested just beside the hole and then they went inside for the evening.

That night Julia once again heard the scampering of little feet. The next morning, when she got up, she rushed outside. She climbed the ladder to see the trap and there he was—a small, frightened squirrel, huddled in the corner of the trap, surrounded by apple seeds and small ragged bits of peel. She called her parents and they came out to take the trap down.

Father said, "We'd better take him far away from here. Do you want to go with me, Julia?"

Julia climbed in the jeep with the cage at her feet. As they bumped along on the old logging road, the squirrel was completely still. Julia could feel his fear as they reached the end of the road and got out of the jeep. Father set the cage down on the ground under a tree and opened the doors. He waited for the squirrel to come out, but he didn't move. He just crouched trembling in the cage, watching furtively with his dark eyes.

Father picked up the cage and turned it upside down. "Hey, fella, you have to come out of there." He shook the cage. The squirrel clung to the wires with his claws, but finally Father shook so hard that he came tumbling out onto the ground. He lay there motionless for a few moments and Julia wondered if he was dead. She could see a trace of blood on his mouth where he had tried to chew his way out of the cage. She wanted to comfort him, but she knew she'd only frighten him more. Suddenly, as she watched, he gave a little lurch and turned over on his stomach.

"He'll be fine," Father said. "Come on, Julia, let's go."

They drove back to the cabin in silence. When they got there, Mother came out and started helping Father put the new wire around the eaves. Julia went inside and sat down on her bed, thinking about the little squirrel. She lay back on her pillow, staring at the ceiling and listening to the sound of the hammer as her parents put the wire up. She closed her eyes. She was getting sleepy. Her mind drifted up towards the ceiling where she had first heard the squirrel. She felt herself reach the boards of the ceiling and pass right through them as though they were made of air. Above the boards she saw the

insulation—dense yellow fiberglass fuzz, soft and prickly at the same time. It was dark up above the ceiling and there wasn't much room. The boards were nailed to one side of the rafters and the roof was nailed to the other side. There was just enough space to huddle deep in the insulation and listen to the banging of the hammer as the wire went up to bar the entrance to the ceiling—and the exit from it.

Julia sat up in bed. "The exit from it," she said softly to herself. Then she jumped out of bed and ran outside, calling, "Mother, Father, wait. Don't put all the wire up. There's another squirrel and she's in there now."

Mother looked down at her from the ladder. "Did you hear her?" she asked.

"Well, not exactly, but yes, kind of …" Julia stopped because she could see that her mother was giving her that strange look again.

"Well," Father said, "We're almost done, but I guess we'll have to set the trap and finish this last section tomorrow."

The next day Julia ran outside, expecting to see another squirrel in the trap, but this time it was empty—completely empty—even the apple was gone. That night Mother re-set the trap, wiring the apple down even more securely, but the next morning it was gone again and the trap was empty. For the next several days, Mother and Father took turns thinking of new ways to set the trap, but each time the squirrel outwitted them. Finally, one sunny afternoon in late October, Mother said, "It's so warm. If that squirrel doesn't come out of the ceiling today, she never will."

That afternoon, Julia went to her bedroom and lay down on her bed. She closed her eyes and let her mind drift up to the ceiling again. She searched every corner of that dark space between the ceiling and the roof, but she couldn't find the squirrel. Then she got up and went out into the kitchen where Mother and Father were cutting up vegetables for soup. She said, "You can finish putting the wire up. The squirrel isn't there."

Her parents looked at her and then at each other. Mother said, "All right, Jack. Let's go," and they went outside to finish the wire.

After that, they heard the squirrel come every night and scurry around on the roof, trying to find her way back in. One night in late November, the wind turned sharp and cold and a thick sleet began to fall. Julia lay in her bed and waited for the squirrel. She knew when she came even before she started scratching on a corner of the roof, trying to find her way back into that cozy dark place. Julia could feel her desperation. Winter was coming and the squirrel had not prepared another nest. She was counting on the insulation. Julia could feel her tremble as the sharp sleet struck against her thick fur. Julia began to cry.

After a few minutes, Mother heard her and came in to see what was wrong. She put her arm around Julia and listened as she cried about the squirrel. "She's so cold and that was her baby we took down the logging road. It just isn't fair that we're warm and dry and she has no place to go."

Mother stayed until Julia stopped crying and then she went out into the other room. Julia heard her pull back a chair and sit down at the table. She heard Father say, "So?"

Mother said softly, "Jack, that child is getting stranger and stranger. I think we'd better find her a friend—an actual human friend her own age, for a change."

4.

Gabriel

In December, the snow came. It snowed for days. The forest turned white. The garden was buried. Even the jeep was buried. Father had to dig it out when the snow finally stopped. It was hard to walk anywhere. Father and Mother took turns plowing the logging road with the big tractor. At times, it snowed so heavily that Julia couldn't even go outside. It would be too easy to get lost in the woods. So she stayed inside and did her school work and, when she was done, she read.

One afternoon, she was looking through the book case trying to find something new to read. She picked up a book called *The Portable Emerson*. She looked through it and found that it contained the writings of Ralph Waldo Emerson who lived in the early part of the 19th century. She read a few sentences from an essay called "Nature," which was difficult for her to understand. She was just about to put the book back on the shelf when one sentence caught her attention. "But if a man would be alone, let him look at the stars."

Julia closed the book, leaving her finger to mark the page, and thought about the night a few weeks ago when Father had taken her outside to look at the stars. They had been studying the constellations in science class and he wanted her to see them for herself. The air was cold and the sky was perfectly clear. The leaves were gone from the trees so it was easy to see the sky. Father pointed out the constellations Julia had seen in her science book—Cassiopeia, the little dipper circling the North Star, the Pleiades, and the hunter Orion with the dog star Sirius.

"See how bright Sirius is," Father said. "That's the brightest star in the heavens."

"No, look, Father. There's another really bright star. It's as bright as Sirius." Julia pointed to the sky above the cabin roof.

"That isn't a star. See, it isn't twinkling like the others."

Julia looked. "It's true. It isn't twinkling. It's bright and steady. What is it?" she asked.

"It's a planet—Jupiter, the biggest planet in the solar system. Remember, you saw a picture of it. When we get the telescope we just ordered, you'll be able to see some of its moons."

Julia stood on the frozen ground and gazed up at the stars. Father didn't speak again. He was looking, too. She almost forgot he was there. The sky was so big and she was so small. She felt like she was the only person in the universe, but it wasn't a scary feeling because somehow she was connected to all those sparkling points of light. She stood and looked at the stars for a long time.

"It's getting cold. Let's go in now and have some hot tea."

Father's voice seemed to come from far away. Julia had to shake herself to bring her attention back to earth. She had gone inside then to drink tea with Father and Mother, but she hadn't forgotten the way it felt to stand there and gaze up at the stars. And now, she was holding in her hand the writing of someone who had lived over a hundred years ago and who had seen those stars the same way she had.

She brought the book to her mother and said, "Mother, I want to read 'Nature,' but I don't understand all of it. Can we read it for school? That way you can help me with it."

Mother smiled. "Emerson," she said thoughtfully, picking up the book. "I read that in university. I liked Emerson. He made me think. Yes, let's give it a try."

Reading Emerson was hard, but Julia persisted. She looked up words in the dictionary and listened carefully as Mother explained the more difficult passages. When she went outside into the forest, she remembered things that Emerson had written. "Nature always wears the colours of the spirit." This meant that the forest reflected the way Julia felt when she looked at it. When she was happy, she saw the sunshine sparkling on the snow. When she was sad, she saw the deep shadows under the huge rocks piled at the foot of the cliff.

One day she skied over to the old maple and stood for a long time gazing up at his broad trunk and snow-covered branches. "What do I see when I look at him?" she asked herself.

She skied around to the other side of the tree where the branch had fallen off. She knew that under the snow there was a large crack in one of the other branches. It would fall some day, too. That thought made her sad. The tree was old. Like her grandfather, he would not live forever. She saw old age and death and she shivered.

Then she looked up, way up, to the top branches. They were so far up they seemed to touch the sky. They reached out in all directions. Julia saw chickadees hopping from one long branch to another. She saw the generosity of the tree and his wisdom. She felt comforted. She looked at the markings on the trunk where the porcupine had scraped away the bark and the woodpeckers had tapped little holes. There were lines, too, made by insects that formed strange patterns as if something had been written there in secret code. Julia saw the mystery of the tree and the lessons she was learning from him. She turned and skied away, back to the cabin. For once, she felt that she didn't need to ask him anything.

That night, when she went to bed, Julia thought again about the question the tree had asked her back in June—"Who are you really?" She reviewed all the possibilities she'd thought of to explain her secret identity—a princess, a refugee from an exotic country, even a child from another planet like the boy in *Le Petit Prince*, which she'd read last year for French class. These were just fantasies and she knew it—fun to think about, but not at all what the tree had in mind.

Then she remembered that the tree had told her that everything she needed would come in time. That had been his response when she'd said she wanted someone to talk to. She realized that he could have said, "Well, you can talk to me," but he didn't. He knew what she meant. She needed a friend, a human friend, preferably someone her own age, who would understand her. She had been patient for a long time now. Mentally, she counted the months that had passed since that conversation—six months—she'd been patient for six months. "Isn't it time now?" she asked into the darkness of her room. She was still waiting for an answer when she fell asleep.

A few weeks after Christmas, Father came bursting into the cabin after his weekly trip down to the campground. "Irene, Julia," he called. "Tomorrow, we're going on a family outing."

"Where?" Julia and Mother asked in unison. It was rare that they went on outings because there was so much work to do in the forest.

"We're going down to the campground. There's a new manager there and he has a son around Julia's age. They've just moved here from Ontario." Mother nodded and smiled.

Julia stared at her father for a few seconds and then she walked over to the window. She looked out at the snowy woods. She could see deep into the forest because there were no leaves on the trees to block her view. The sky was cloudy and there were a few snowflakes falling through the still air. The woods were so quiet in the winter. She felt a strange tightening in her throat as she thought about meeting a boy her own age. She closed her eyes for a moment and heard a voice inside her mind say softly, "He's your brother."

She opened her eyes, startled. She turned around to face the room and Father said, "What's the matter, Julia, don't you want to meet someone your age?"

"I don't know," Julia said. She paused a moment and then said, "Well, yes, I guess I do."

"Good." Father smiled. "Then it's all set. We'll leave tomorrow morning, right after breakfast."

After lunch that day, Julia asked her mother if she could take a break from her studies. Mother said yes and Julia quickly put on her snowsuit. She went out to the shed behind the cabin to get her skis. She put them on and glided down the path from the cabin. She knew exactly where she was going. She had recognized the voice that had spoken in her mind that morning. She skied straight to the old maple tree and stopped underneath his branches. She took a few deep breaths to quiet her mind and then said, "Why did you say he's my brother? I don't have a brother." She closed her eyes and stood there, waiting for an answer.

There were several minutes of silence and then slowly the words began to form in her mind. "Of course, you have a brother—they're all your brothers, really."

"All who?" asked Julia.

"All the other people—your brothers and your sisters."

"Then why did you say that this boy in particular is my brother?"

"Because there are agreements made beforehand."

"Before what? This doesn't make any sense."

"Actually, it isn't really a case of before or after—because there isn't any before or after if time is only an illusion—but there are agreements made."

"You're getting me confused again. You mean I've made an agreement with someone I've never met? How is that possible?"

"How is it possible to be in the mind of a bird or a squirrel when you aren't either one of them right now?"

"Hmm," Julia said thoughtfully. "You have a point. I suppose this is one of those things that will become clear later on."

"Yes, one would hope so."

Julia stood there a few more minutes, but the tree was silent so she turned around and headed back to the cabin.

The next morning the weather was cold and clear. Julia and her parents quickly ate breakfast and packed some food to take to share with the campground manager and his son. They drove down the old logging road laughing and talking, excited by the novelty of going on an outing together. When they reached the campground, however, Julia fell silent. She felt nervous about meeting new people—especially this mysterious boy with whom she supposedly had made an agreement.

Julia and her parents got out of the jeep and walked across the parking area of the campground to the small house where the manager lived. Father knocked on the door and Julia heard a deep voice say, "Come in."

She stayed behind her parents as Father opened the door and walked in. Julia stepped into the house just behind him and closed the door. She looked around the room. It was small, even smaller than the main room of the cabin, which was both kitchen and living room for Julia's family. The walls of this room were painted white unlike the cabin whose walls were unfinished spruce tongue-in-groove. Peering around from behind her father, Julia could see a wood stove in the far corner of the room and a small table next to a window. There was a multi-coloured braided rug on the worn wooden floor. She saw an old rocking chair in another corner and a green couch beside the window opposite the table. A tall man with curly hair and a thick brown beard rose from the chair as her father greeted him.

"Hello, Sam," Father said. "I've brought the family and some food for lunch."

"Hi, Jack, and welcome to all of you," said the man named Sam. Julia liked his voice. It was warm and rumbly and sounded as though he might start laughing at any moment.

"This is Irene, my wife, and Julia, my daughter." Father stepped out of the way so Julia could be seen.

"How do you do?" Sam stepped forward to shake hands with Julia's mother. "And how are you, young lady?" he said, looking down at Julia with a broad smile. His eyes were bright and twinkly and Julia returned his smile in spite of her nervousness. "I have someone I'd like you to meet." Sam turned toward the other room and called through the open door, "Gabe, come out here."

Julia held her breath as the slight figure of a young boy around her age appeared in the doorway. "This is Gabriel, my son," Sam said.

Gabriel raised his eyes to look at Julia and then lowered them quickly. "Hello," he said softly.

"Hello." Julia looked at Gabriel intently for a few seconds before lowering her eyes as he had done. She saw immediately that he looked nothing like his father. Sam was tall and robust with blue eyes and a ruddy complexion. Gabriel was slender and almost frail with straight black hair, dark olive skin and deep brown eyes.

"He doesn't look anything like me, either," thought Julia. "I have wavy brown hair and blue eyes and I think I might even be taller than he is." She realized she had half expected this boy to look like her twin after what the tree had told her.

There was a moment of silence and then Sam said, "Well, Jack and Irene, would you like to take a tour of the camp? I'll fill you in on some plans I have for improving the facilities.

Maybe Gabriel could show your daughter around. He's been exploring the woods ever since we got here."

Julia's parents nodded in agreement and the grownups left. Neither Julia nor Gabriel moved as the door closed, leaving them alone together. Julia thought, "He feels as uncomfortable as I do."

Finally, Gabriel cleared his throat and said, "Do you go to school?"

"At home with my parents. I'm in secondary two—grade nine."

"So am I. I go at home now, too, since we've moved here."

"Do you like it?"

"Yes, I never really cared for school. They always said I didn't talk enough in class."

"Me, too. Same thing. On my report cards it always said, 'Julia does well on her tests, but she needs to participate more in class.'" She told herself, "We do have something in common even if we don't look alike."

There was a moment of awkward silence and finally Gabriel said, "Well, do you want to go outside?"

"OK."

Gabriel put on his coat and boots and Julia followed him out the door. The sun was shining brightly, but the air was still cold. Julia and Gabriel walked down the path that led across the clearing and into the woods. Neither one spoke. They could see their parents on the other side of the clearing, inspecting the playground area. As they walked into the woods, the snow became deeper and they had to walk slowly. Julia said, "We need snowshoes."

"There are some back at the house. Should we go get them?"

"No, not now." Julia felt more comfortable outside in the woods and Gabriel seemed more relaxed, too. She followed him as he led her down a path which curved around behind a small cliff. At the bottom of the cliff there were several large rocks which had fallen, one on top of the other, forming a natural cave.

Gabriel pointed to the cave. "An animal lives in there. I saw him once. It looked like a porcupine."

"Is he there now?"

"No."

"How can you tell? Do you know when he's there and when he's gone?"

"Yes." Gabriel paused for a moment and then said, "I can feel it."

Julia nodded.

Gabriel pointed to a steep, snow-covered path that led up the side of the cliff and asked, "Do you think you could climb up there?"

"Yes, of course." Julia followed Gabriel as he started climbing. The snow was deep and the climb was difficult, but it was worth it when they reached the top. They were at the edge of a large pine grove. When they looked down from the cliff, they could see deep into the woods where the snow sparkled like diamonds in the sunshine.

"It's beautiful," said Julia.

"Yes, I come here often."

They stood in silence for a few minutes, looking out at the snow and the trees. Then Julia turned to Gabriel and said, "You don't look much like your father."

"No, I look like my mother's side of the family. She was born in India."

"Is she in India now?"

"No. She left the body two years ago."

"Do you mean she died?" Julia knew she was asking too many personal questions, but she simply had to know.

"Yes, you could say that, but she didn't believe in death."

"What did she believe in?"

"She believed in life. She believed in God."

"Do you miss her?"

"Yes, sometimes, but ..." Gabriel paused.

"But what?"

Gabriel turned and looked at Julia intently. "Can you keep a secret?"

"Yes," Julia said solemnly.

"Well, I see her sometimes. She talks to me."

"What do you mean, she talks to you? Do you hear her out loud? Do you see her with your eyes open?"

"No, with my eyes closed and I hear her voice in my mind."

"Oh. I understand."

"You do?"

"Yes," Julia said. "There's someone that talks to me like that, too."

"Who?"

"A tree."

"A tree? What kind of tree?"

"An old maple. He gives me advice." Julia looked at Gabriel. "Do you think I'm crazy?"

"No. I don't think you're crazy. Trees have souls, too, so why shouldn't they talk?"

"I never told anyone else about the tree."

"I never told anyone else about my mother."

"Not even your dad?"

"Especially not my dad. It makes him too sad to talk about her. He really misses her."

"I understand," Julia said again.

They stood for a few moments and looked out at the forest. The wind came and Julia shivered. "We'd better go back," Gabriel said. "It's getting colder." He turned toward the pine grove and said, "We can go this way. It's faster and we don't have to go back down the cliff."

They walked in silence through the snow until they came to the edge of the clearing. When they reached the house, Gabriel opened the door. "Our parents aren't back yet. They must be over at the community center. Come on. I'll show you a picture of my mother."

Julia followed Gabriel into the house. They took off their coats and boots and he went into his room. She watched from the doorway as he took a picture down from the top of a large book case filled with books.

"You like to read," Julia said.

"Yes, do you?"

"Of course."

Gabriel handed her the picture. Julia saw a woman with dark skin, dressed in a white robe. She had a white scarf draped loosely over her black hair. "She's beautiful."

"Yes. Her name is Mira, which means 'the beautiful one.'"

"It suits her. She has a nice smile, too."

"I know. When I see her now, she's always smiling."

Suddenly Julia heard Sam's voice outside. Gabriel took the picture quickly out of her hands and put it back on the book case just as the door opened.

"Time for lunch," Sam said as he walked in with Julia's parents. "Did you go for a walk?"

"Yes," Gabriel said.

"It was nice," Julia added.

After lunch, everyone sat and drank peppermint tea for a while until Mother said, "We really have to be getting back. We still have things to do today."

They put on their coats and boots. As they started out the door, Julia turned and said, "Good bye, Gabriel."

He walked up to her and said, "Good bye." Then he looked at his father, who was laughing with Julia's parents. He stepped closer to Julia and whispered, "I'd like to meet your tree some time."

"Yes," Julia replied and she followed her parents out the door.

5.

Sister and Brother

On the drive back to the cabin, Julia was quiet. At first her mother tried to draw her out. She asked, "Did you like Gabriel?"

"Yes."

"What did the two of you do?"

"Walked in the woods."

"What did you talk about?"

"Nothing much."

At that point, Mother gave up and left Julia alone with her thoughts in the back seat of the jeep. Julia realized that her mother probably thought she was upset, but she wasn't. She just needed time to think about everything that had happened that day. "So," she asked herself, "what exactly has happened? I've finally met someone who understands me, that's all."

Once again, she heard the voice of the tree saying, "He's your brother," and she felt a little thrill of fear deep down in the center of her happiness. She knew she'd been guarding her secrets closely and she didn't know what it would be like to finally share them. She hadn't told Gabriel that the tree had said he was her brother. She still felt too shy. She suspected he wouldn't be surprised, though.

The next morning, Julia woke up to find another blizzard howling outside the cabin. She had planned to go talk to the tree as soon as she finished her chores. She had some questions she wanted answered. She looked outside the window of her bedroom and saw that the snow was blowing so heavily she couldn't even see the shed where she kept her skis. She ate breakfast and did the dishes. Then she went back to her bedroom with a book, resigned to waiting out the storm. From time to time, throughout the day, she went to the window to gaze out at the sky. She hoped to see some sign of the storm dying down, but the snow continued to fall and the wind continued to blow. Julia finally went to bed that night with her questions unanswered.

The next morning, when she woke up, it was still dark out, but she couldn't hear the wind anymore. She hoped this meant that the storm was over. Her bedroom door was partly open and she could see the light of the lamp in the kitchen as her parents started the fire and made breakfast. It was cold in her room so she stayed in bed until she could hear the fire crackling in the wood stove. Then she jumped out of bed, dressed quickly and went out to the kitchen.

Julia huddled close to the stove as her father went out to get some more firewood. When he came back in, he said, "It must have snowed a foot yesterday. The jeep is covered again." The sky was just beginning to lighten, and Julia looked out the window to the clearing where the jeep was parked. All she could see was a white mound. The storm was definitely over, however, and the sky was clear. She saw Venus shining brightly in the east against the rosy glow that was deepening behind the bare branches of the trees.

Julia ate her breakfast quickly, did the dishes and then got out her school books. She tried to concentrate on her lessons, but she was still thinking about Gabriel when her break time came. She put on her ski suit and hurried down the path her father had shovelled to the shed. She got her skis and then plowed her way through the thick snow until she reached the old maple tree. She had thought of many questions concerning Gabriel and his mother, but when she found herself standing beneath the broad branches of the tree, she simply asked, "Should I bring him here to meet you?"

She paused and let the stillness of the winter woods fill her mind as she waited for the tree's answer. When it came, it was as she expected—"Yes, bring him." Julia skied back to the cabin, wondering how she could arrange for Gabriel to come meet the tree.

When she came in the cabin door, lunch was ready and Julia sat down at the table. Her mind wandered as her parents talked about several projects they were planning to do in the spring. She was eating slowly and gazing out the window when she suddenly realized her mother had just asked her a question. Julia looked up and said, "I'm sorry. I wasn't listening. What did you say?"

"I said that your father and I were talking about the possibility of asking Sam and Gabriel over for next Saturday. Would you like that?"

"Saturday? Yes, yes I would."

"OK, we'll call them tonight."

So that night Father called Sam and made arrangements for the next Saturday. Sam said they would bring their skis and something to share for lunch. When Julia went to bed that night, she lay awake for a long time thinking about how to introduce Gabriel to the tree.

Sam and Gabriel came around ten Saturday morning. The weather was warmer than it had been the week-end before. The sky was cloudy and a light snow was falling. When Gabriel arrived, Julia felt shy again and she could tell that he did, too. They sat and drank peppermint tea with the grownups, listening to Julia's parents discuss a problem they'd had with hunters in the fall.

Father said, "I know that the fence is down along the back section of the property and I think they're using that as an excuse to come in even though there are No Hunting signs posted all along the fence line."

Sam said, "Maybe in the spring I can get away from the camp for a while and help you make some repairs."

Mother said, "That would be great. It's hard with just the two of us."

Father said, "I'll ask Dr. La Tendresse's agent if we can hire Réjean, too."

"Who's Réjean?" Sam asked.

"He's a handyman who does odd jobs here from time to time. He's educated though and perfectly bilingual. I think he said he was a retired school teacher. He's a bit strange—doesn't say much—but he's a good worker."

Julia looked at Gabriel, who was sitting on the other side of his father. "Did you bring your skis?" she asked.

"Yes, they're out in the truck."

"Then, let's go."

They excused themselves and headed for the door. They

put on their skis and started down the path. This time, Gabriel followed Julia. At the end of the path where it turned onto the old logging road, she stopped and turned to look at him. "I asked him if I could bring you."

"What did he say?"

"He said yes."

Gabriel smiled. "I'm ready."

It didn't take long to reach the tree. Julia skied under his branches and Gabriel followed her. Then she took off her skis and stood in the deep snow with her back leaning against the broad trunk of the tree. Gabriel did the same. They both looked up through the branches and saw the sun peeking through a cloud. Julia said, "You have to be very still and it helps to close your eyes."

"All right." Gabriel shut his eyes.

Julia said in a soft voice, "This is Gabriel. I brought him to meet you." Then she closed her eyes and waited for the thoughts of the tree to enter her mind.

They stood quietly for several moments until they heard the wind come up from the valley behind the cabin with a gentle sighing sound. At that moment the silent voice of the tree said, "You will have much to do—you and your sister." Julia opened her eyes, surprised that the tree had talked to Gabriel first. She saw that Gabriel's eyes were still shut so she closed hers again and listened.

She thought she could hear Gabriel saying, "So, I do have a sister," but she knew he hadn't spoken out loud.

She felt her own thoughts reaching out to the tree. "What do we have to do?"

"You will know when the time comes, but don't clutter your mind too much. Stay receptive."

Julia waited to see if there were any further messages, but there was nothing except the sound of the wind and a few dry leaves rattling against a branch. Julia opened her eyes and looked at Gabriel.

"Did you hear him?" she asked. She held her breath as she waited for his answer.

"Yes. He said you are my sister and that we have much to do."

Julia let her breath out with a sigh of relief. "So it isn't just my imagination. Or, at any rate, if I'm crazy, you must be, too."

"No, we're not crazy."

"What did you mean when you said, 'So I do have a sister?'"

"Well," Gabriel said slowly, "my mother told me once that I had a sister, but a spiritual sister, not a biological sister. That's how she put it and she said I would meet her some day."

"What does that mean—a spiritual sister?"

"I think it has to do with past lives."

"Past lives?"

"Yes, my mother said that we've had other lives before this one."

"The tree said something like that once, too. He said that we'd made an agreement."

"An agreement to do what?"

"I don't know. Maybe to do whatever it is he was talking about today."

"Evidently, there's a lot we don't know yet," Gabriel said. "I suppose it will all be revealed in time and we have to be patient."

"I'm getting tired of being patient."

"Well, I don't see that we have much choice."

Julia and Gabriel put their skis on and started back up the trail that Julia had made alongside the old logging road. They skied past the cabin, following the road as it led deep into the forest. They didn't pause until they reached a large clearing in the middle of the woods.

"The fence isn't far from here," Julia said.

"Is that where it's down?"

"That's one of the places. There are several."

"Do you think that fixing the fence will keep the hunters out?"

"I don't know. Maybe it will help at least."

"Do you see many deer around here?"

"There are deer all over the woods."

"We don't see them often down by the camp. I guess there are too many people."

"Probably."

They stood for a moment and looked at the clearing. There

were still traces of some of the trees that had been cut down. Many had been left lying on the ground and their branches protruded through the snow.

Then Julia looked at Gabriel and said, "You, know, I always wanted a brother or a sister."

"So did I. It's hard sometimes being an only child."

"You don't think we're just making it up—about being brother and sister?"

"Well, both my mother and the tree said it, didn't they?"

"Yes, I guess they know. But, Gabriel," Julia had a sudden thought, "how do they know? The tree knows about everything I do. He even knew about the dead leaf."

"What dead leaf?"

"When I first noticed him—before he ever talked to me— he dropped a leaf on my head. I took it to my room and put it in a box."

"Why did you do that?"

"I don't know. It seemed significant—and mysterious. It was like he meant for that leaf to go on my head—like it was a message or something."

"So how do you know he knew you kept it?"

"Because the first time he talked to me, he told me I could throw it away—that I didn't need it anymore."

"And did you?"

"Yes, I dumped it in the woods."

"Hmm." Gabriel paused. Then he said, "Julia, do you know why your parents didn't have any more children?"

"No, but I think they tried once. I was small—maybe four years old. I used to listen to them talking at night when they thought I was asleep. Actually, I still do. Anyway, I heard them talking about a baby and they sounded happy. Then one day, my mother went away. She was gone all night and the next night, when she came back, I heard them talking again. My mother was crying, and my father said, 'We can always have another one.' But they didn't. I don't know why. How about your parents?"

"My mother got sick. She was sick for a long time. That was sad, too." Gabriel looked around at the clearing again.

"Why were all the trees cut down here?" he asked.

"I don't know. They must have been cut before the rich doctor bought the property. He won't let anyone cut live trees. It looks strange, doesn't it? Almost like a battle ground." Julia stood silent for a few minutes, picturing men in sturdy boots with their big saws, cutting down the beautiful trees, one by one. She sighed and said, "I guess we'd better head back. I think it's almost lunchtime."

6.

Tapping

Winter lasted for a long time. It snowed and snowed. Julia and Gabriel made ski trails through the woods and each week it seemed they had to remake them because they were once again covered with new snow. They also went out with their snowshoes to gather dead branches for kindling, stopping often to talk to the old maple tree. It was fun for a while, but by the end of February, Julia was getting tired of winter. "Will the snow never end?" she complained, looking out the window at another storm.

"Soon enough," Father said. "We have a lot to do once the thaw comes."

Then early one Saturday morning in March, Julia woke up to the sound of rain on the cabin roof. "Rain," she cried, jumping out of bed. She ran to the window. "It's raining. The snow will melt. Spring is coming."

She pulled on her clothes and ran out to the kitchen. Father was just coming in the door with an armload of firewood. "Father, spring is coming. We have to tap the maple trees."

Father laughed. "We have to wait until the rain stops and the nights turn cold again. Warm days—cold nights. That's what makes the sap run."

"Do you think it will snow again?"

"The radio says this will turn to snow tonight."

"Oh, no. I'm tired of snow."

"Everybody is by this time of year, but we don't get a vote where the weather's concerned." Father put some wood in the stove. "We have to move fast as soon as the weather clears. We want to fix up the sugar cabin so we can tap more trees this year. Sam's going to help us."

"Really? We won't boil it down in the cabin anymore?"

"No, we can only do a few trees that way. We'd like to make enough to share with Sam and Gabriel."

"Speaking of Gabriel, I'd better call him. We were supposed to go skiing today, but the snow will be too wet."

"Sam is coming over to look at the sugar cabin. Maybe he can bring Gabriel and you can do something else."

"Good idea. I'll call right now."

Sam and Gabriel arrived right after lunch. Sam and Julia's parents left immediately to go look at the sugar cabin. The rain had let up, but the sky was still cloudy. Julia put on her boots and went outside with Gabriel.

"Where should we go?" she asked.

"The snow's so soft, we'll have to stay on the road. It's impossible to walk anywhere else."

So Julia and Gabriel walked up the logging road toward the fence line. The wind started to blow and Julia wrapped her scarf tighter around her neck. "It's getting colder. My dad says it's going to snow again."

"That's what I heard." Gabriel pulled his gloves out of his pockets and put them on. When they reached the end of the road, they stood a moment and looked toward the fence, which was still down in places. "I have to tell you something," Gabriel said.

"What?"

"My mother came this morning."

"Came where?"

"To my room—just as I was waking up."

"Did you see her?"

"Yes, but still with my eyes closed."

"What did she say?"

"She said I should try to clear my mind."

"How?"

"She said I should meditate."

"Meditate? How do you do that?"

"She showed me once. She and my dad used to meditate together every morning. They just sat still with their eyes closed. Since they were doing it, I wanted to do it, too, so she told me to sit down and cross my legs. Then she said to close my eyes and say OM to myself over and over while I watched my breath go in and out."

"OM? What does that mean?"

"It's just a sound—a sacred sound. It's like the sound of creation."

"I don't understand."

"Well, I guess I don't either. Anyway, I did it for a while, but then I got bored and stopped. When my mother died, my dad stopped, too. I guess it reminded him of her."

"So are you going to try it again?"

"I suppose so. Will you do it, too?"

"I can try—maybe tonight after I go to bed—just say OM and watch my breath. That doesn't sound too complicated."

"No. Then she said something else."

"Your mother?"

"Yes. She said, 'Don't tap the old maple tree.'"

"What?" Julia looked at Gabriel in astonishment.

"Don't tap the old maple tree. But I don't understand what she's talking about. Tap him with our fingers? We don't do that anyway."

"No—not with our fingers—with the spiles."

"The what?"

"The little spouts they put in the trees to collect the sap for maple syrup. We've been making some every year, but we've only tapped a few trees right around the cabin because we didn't have any place to boil it down. Now my father says we're going to fix up the sugar cabin so we can tap a lot of trees. That's why your dad is here today—to look at it."

"Even our tree?"

"I don't know. Probably. He's right in the middle of the maple grove."

"But we have to stop them."

"How? If we ask them not to, they'll want to know why. I wonder why your mother said he shouldn't be tapped."

"Maybe because it would take away his energy."

"Oh, no, that would be terrible. He wouldn't be able to talk to us anymore."

"Well, we really have to stop them then. We have to think of a way."

That evening, after dinner, Julia went to her room with a book. She had to leave her door open so the heat from the stove could reach her. She sat on her bed reading until her parents turned off the light in the kitchen and went to their room. Then she quietly got up and lit a candle and turned off the light. She sat up straight on her bed and crossed her legs. She closed her eyes and started thinking OM each time she breathed in and each time she breathed out.

Julia could hear the wind outside the cabin. It was even stronger now than it had been during the day. She continued breathing and saying OM to herself while she listened to the wind. It was like her breath, the air moving in and out, through the branches of the trees, around the corners of the cabin. It was like the universe breathing. Julia listened and felt herself flying with the wind through the forest. With her eyes still tightly closed, she could see the tops of the trees with their bare branches.

Then she saw the maple grove and the old tree standing in the middle across the road from the sugar cabin. She felt the wind rattle his branches. Inside he was quiet, but down below the snow, where his roots reached deep into the earth, something was beginning to stir. "The sap. It won't be long now." Julia's mind spoke the thought over the sound of the OM. She could feel the pulling at the deep ends of the roots. The urgency of life was still there, but she knew it wasn't as strong as it once had been. Gabriel was right. The tree would need all the energy he could get. She opened her eyes and stretched out her legs. "He mustn't be tapped," she told herself. "He mustn't. We have to think of a plan."

The next week it rained again and this time it didn't turn to snow. It rained for two days and two nights and the snow began to melt. Julia and Gabriel went to town with their parents to buy the materials for repairing the sugar cabin. They also bought more buckets and spiles and extra batteries for the drill. Toward the end of the week, the sun came out and the temperature slowly began to climb. During the day, the snow that was left was wet and soggy. At night it froze again and in the morning there was a crust of ice on top.

Saturday morning when Julia came out to breakfast, Mother said, "Today's the day. The sap is sure to run today."

"Are Sam and Gabriel coming over?"

"Yes, they'll be here right after breakfast. We'll go hang the buckets and then do the work on the sugar cabin."

When Julia finished washing the breakfast dishes, she went back to her room. She pulled a sweat shirt out of her dresser and put it on. Then she went to her closet. Quickly, she dug through a small box of her old toys until she found what she wanted—a small piece of yellow modelling clay. She wrapped it in a piece of plastic and put it in her pocket.

"Are you ready, Julia?" Mother called. "Sam and Gabriel are here."

"Coming."

Julia went back to the kitchen and picked up a stack of buckets, which were sitting on the counter with their lids. Mother was holding the drill with the extra batteries and a plastic bag with the spiles. As they left the cabin, Gabriel looked at Julia anxiously. "What are we going to do?" he whispered.

"Don't worry. I have a plan."

When they reached the maple trees, Mother drilled the first hole. It was difficult cutting through the hard maple wood so everyone took turns as they went from tree to tree. People also took turns hammering in the spiles and hanging the buckets. The sun was already shining on the trees and some of them started dripping even as the spiles went in. Julia caught some of the sap on her finger and put it in her mouth. She liked the taste of the maple water. It was fresh and cool and slightly sweet. When she drank it, she felt a communion with the tree that had given it.

When they finally came to the old maple, Father started to drill the hole.

"Don't you think this tree's too old to tap?" Julia asked.

"Oh, we can give it a try. We'll just put one in and see if it gives."

Gabriel looked at Julia again. She could see the anxiety in his eyes. She didn't say anything. As she watched Father make the hole, she could almost feel the bit of the drill cutting into the trunk of the tree. Mother hammered in the spile. At first there was no sap and then a couple of drops fell slowly into the bucket.

"Maybe this tree is too old," Mother said.

Gabriel looked hopeful.

"Oh, it might pick up as the sun gets warmer. Come on. Let's get finished so we have time to do the sugar cabin." Father picked up the last two buckets and headed for another tree where Sam was already drilling the hole.

Julia stayed a moment beside the tree. Gabriel came up to her and said softly, "I thought you had a plan."

"I do, but I have to wait a bit. The sap isn't coming fast. I don't think he'll lose too much."

As soon as the last two trees were tapped, everyone went to the sugar cabin. The materials for the repairs were already there. Father handed Julia and Gabriel hammers and a sack of nails. "Here," he said. "I'll cut the boards for the back wall and you two can hammer them in."

They worked for a little over an hour and then Mother said, "It's almost noon. I'm going to heat up the soup. You can all come for lunch in fifteen minutes."

They put up a few more boards and then Father said, "OK, that's it. Lunch time."

"Go ahead," Julia said. "I'll just finish nailing this board."

Gabriel looked at her and she whispered, "Go with them. It will be less obvious if I do this by myself."

"What are you going to do?"

"I'll explain later."

So Gabriel followed Father and Sam to the cabin. Julia continued hammering until they were out of sight. Then she put down the nails and, still holding her hammer, she ran across the road to the old maple tree. She knew she had to work fast. She took down the bucket and pried the spile out with her hammer. Then she took the modelling clay out of her pocket and pulled off a little piece. She stuffed it into the end of the spile where it went into the tree. Quickly, she hammered the spile back in and hung the bucket. She watched for a moment to be sure no drops of sap came through the spile. Finally, she smiled and patted the trunk of the tree. "There," she said. "The rest is up to you. Send the sap wherever you need it."

Julia ran back across the road to the sugar cabin. She hammered the last nail in the board and then ran up to the cabin for lunch.

Once they knew their tree was protected, Julia and Gabriel enjoyed making the syrup. They went from tree to tree checking the buckets and taking little sips of maple water. They always stopped by the old maple to make sure there was no sap in his bucket.

"How did you think of the modelling clay?" Gabriel asked one morning as he took the bucket down and turned it over to dump out a spider and two beetles.

"Well, after I went to bed one night last week, I was lying there thinking about how we had to stop our parents from tapping our tree. I was making up reasons that might convince them, going over and over them in my mind. I was almost asleep when I heard a voice say, 'Stop up the hole.'"

"Whose voice?"

"I don't know. Maybe it was just my own mind, but it sounded like a voice—not the tree's voice though."

"Was it a grown-up?"

"Yes, I think so—a woman's voice, now that you mention it."

Gabriel looked at Julia with big eyes. "I knew it," he whispered. "It was my mother."

"Your mother? Why would she talk to me?"

"Why shouldn't she? She's the one who warned us not to tap the tree."

"That's true. Gabriel, this is almost spooky." Julia shivered.

"I know. It's like we're being guided." Gabriel looked up at the branches of the tree. "So, anyway, she said to stop up the hole—and then?"

"I guess I fell asleep. The next couple of days I kept thinking about what I could use to stop up the hole. First I was thinking she meant the hole in the tree and I couldn't think of anything that would work. But then, the morning my mom

said we were going to tap, I was doing the dishes and I saw in
my mind the clay stuffed in the end of the spile. I remembered
I had some in my old box of toys so I went in my room and got
it and that's it."

"Oh, look, Julia, your mother's coming."

Julia turned around to see her mother coming down the
road. She was carrying a hammer and the drill. She walked up
to them and said, "I've come to remove the bucket from this
tree. It isn't giving and we might as well put it somewhere else."

"Oh, yes—uh, good idea." Julia could feel Gabriel staring
at her, thinking the same thing she was thinking. If Mother
took out the spile, she'd see the clay.

"Here, Mother. I'll take it out." Julia practically grabbed
the hammer from Mother's hand. "You can go drill the hole in
the other tree."

Mother looked at Julia without speaking. Julia was afraid she
was going to take the hammer back, but Gabriel said quickly,
"Which tree are you going to tap?"

"Oh," Mother said, turning to look at him. "Well, I don't
know." She looked around the maple grove.

"How about that one over there?" Julia pointed. "It has
only one bucket."

"All right," Mother said and headed for the other tree.

"That was close," Gabriel whispered.

Julia quickly removed the spile and pulled the clay plug
from the end of it. "Yes, good thing you distracted her. I hate
having all these secrets, but I know my parents couldn't possibly understand about the tree or about your mother."

"I know. My dad either. Here, give me the spile and the
hammer and I'll take them to your mom."

As Gabriel walked away, Julia leaned against the tree. She
felt relieved that the spile was out. She closed her eyes a
moment. As she stood there, she thought she heard him whis-
per, "Thank you," but it could have been the wind.

7.

The Path

As April drew to a close, even the nights began to be warmer and the maple syrup season came to an end. The last week of April it started raining. It rained steadily for almost an entire week. When the skies finally cleared, the last spots of snow were gone from the shady hollows and the woods were full of puddles. Julia began sleeping with the window open. She could hear the creek from her bedroom as it rushed down its rocky bed and spilled over the banks, unable to contain all the water from the heavy rains and the melting snow.

The last Saturday in May, Julia and Gabriel met on the old logging road halfway between the cabin and the camp ground so they could go for a walk in the woods.

When Julia saw Gabriel, she cried, "Isn't spring wonderful?"

Gabriel smiled. "It's great to go outside without having to put on all those winter things."

"And no more school for three months."

"That's right."

"Gabriel, I had an idea while I was walking here."

"What?"

"Well, there is a much shorter way to go from the cabin to the camp ground. The logging road curves around, but if you go down the ridge that runs behind the cabin and turn to your left, you can cut across that section with the big pines that leads across the creek and straight to the campground. That's the same ridge that turns into the cliff behind the camp, and there's already a big tree lying across the creek which we can use as a bridge."

"How is the terrain?"

"Not bad, but blackberry bushes are in the way in some areas."

"Maybe we could cut ourselves a trail."

"That's what I was thinking."

"Shall we start today?"

"Why not?"

So Julia and Gabriel went to the cabin and got some clippers and a couple of pairs of thick gloves. They climbed down the ridge behind the cabin. As soon as they reached the bottom, they had to start clearing out the berry bushes. They took turns clipping and pulling the cut branches out of the way. They had been working for about an hour when they started to get hungry and thirsty.

As they walked back to the cabin, Julia said, "Tomorrow we should bring some food and water."

Julia and Gabriel worked on their path steadily every day for the rest of the week. They brought snacks and a water bottle in a back pack, which they took turns carrying. At two in the afternoon of the fifth day, they crossed the creek on the fallen tree. Gabriel noted the time on his watch. On the morning of the seventh day, Gabriel met Julia at the cabin as usual.

As he put the water bottle in the back pack, he said, "Today we're going to reach the camp. I feel it."

"I hope you're right. I'm getting really tired of blackberry bushes."

They walked down the ridge to the new path, examining it critically as they went along. Gabriel wanted to stop and trim a little more along the way, but Julia was adamant. "First we finish. Then we can go back and make improvements if we want to."

When they got to the place where they'd stopped the day before, Julia took the clippers and started cutting furiously. Gabriel cleared away the bushes as fast as she could cut. The prospect of finishing gave them energy and they worked in silent efficiency.

They'd been working for two hours when Gabriel suddenly said, "I know this place. We're almost there. As soon as we get through this bunch of berry bushes, we're clear. We just have to walk through another little pine grove and we'll reach the cliff." He checked his watch. "Eleven AM." He took the clippers and started cutting as fast as he could.

Julia grabbed the thorny branches with the leather gloves and flung them to the side. Each time she reached for another branch, she peered ahead, looking for the pine grove. She and Gabriel saw it at the same time. They both cried out, "There it is."

Gabriel said, "Two more cuts and that's it." Julia flung aside the last branches and they stepped onto the soft shady floor of the pine grove. They both stood and looked around for a minute. Gabriel took the pack from his back and pulled out the water bottle. He passed it to Julia first. She took a long drink and passed it back. Then she put the clippers and the gloves in the pack and put it on her back. Gabriel hung the last few ribbons and they walked out of the pine grove, onto the path that zigzagged up the cliff and into the camp. "Twelve noon," he said.

When they reached the camp, they saw Sam standing by the community center talking to another man.

"Who's that?" Gabriel asked.

"Oh, that's Réjean. He's the one who does odd jobs around here sometimes. Maybe your dad's going to hire him to work on the community center."

"Is he the one your dad said is kind of strange?"

"Well, he's strange just because he doesn't say much about himself—or about anything else for that matter."

"He looks pretty old," Gabriel said, looking at Réjean's grey hair and mustache.

"Yes, I guess he's been retired for a while. Come on, let's get something to eat. I'm hungry."

They went into Gabriel's house and Sam joined them a few minutes later. He congratulated them on finishing the path and gave them a sandwich and some cold lemonade.

Gabriel asked, "Dad, are you hiring that man to work on the community center?"

"Réjean? Yes. Julia's father said he was a good worker. Why?"

"Just wondering," Gabriel said.

"Let's walk back through our path now," Julia said, "but no making improvements today. I want to just enjoy it for a change."

"Fine with me." Gabriel took the back pack. They said good bye to Sam and started out.

The path was beautiful. Even Gabriel couldn't find much that needed to be improved. As they walked, Julia thought of what it would be like to take the path in the autumn when the leaves were changing or ski down it in the winter. She said, "I'm so proud of us. We worked really hard."

When they reached the end of the path where it turned to go up the ridge to the cabin, Julia said, "Let's sit for a while."

She pointed to a fallen log and they sat down. Gabriel pulled the water bottle out again and they drank. Then they just sat there, looking around at the forest. The sun was warm and Julia began to feel sleepy. She leaned back against a branch which protruded from the log and closed her eyes. She could feel the darting minds of the birds as they flew from tree to tree. She was also aware of the thin shimmering of the insects and the furtive attention of the tiny toads and mice that hopped and scurried through the wet mat of dead leaves on the forest floor. She felt warm and relaxed and, as she let her mind wander from one creature to another, she slowly became aware of something else—a consciousness, located not far from where she was sitting—a source of gentle, wondering attention, which was directed toward her and Gabriel. She opened her eyes and looked toward the tangle of ferns and blackberries which surrounded a small pine grove not far from where she was sitting.

"Gabriel," she said. "I feel something—there in the bushes."

Gabriel sat up straight and turned in the direction she was pointing. "You're right. Let's go look."

"Yes, but quietly. We don't want to frighten whoever's in there."

Gabriel took a pair of the leather gloves out of the pack. Then they stood up and walked slowly toward the bushes. Gabriel put the gloves on and gently parted the grass and thorns which blocked the entrance to the pine grove. He peered into a small hollow which was partly shaded by the pine trees. "Julia, look."

He stepped back so Julia could see and she gazed down into the hollow. At first she didn't see him because of the spots on his back. He seemed to melt into the grass which was dappled by the sunlight that filtered through the pine trees. She gradually became aware of his eyes. They were dark and almond shaped and they were looking back at her with the same gentle wonder she had sensed when she first noticed his presence.

"Oh. A fawn. He's so beautiful."

"Has he been abandoned?"

"I don't think so. A doe won't abandon her fawn unless something's happened to her. She's probably just out looking for food. But she shouldn't be far away. She wouldn't leave him for too long."

"Maybe we should check back later. I've been hearing coyotes at night. Maybe one of them attacked his mother."

"Maybe. Anyway, we should go away now so she won't be afraid to come back."

They climbed up the ridge to the cabin. "How long should we wait?" Gabriel asked.

"What time is it?"

"Two."

"OK, let's check back at four."

The time passed slowly at the cabin. They helped Julia's parents in the garden for a little while and then went inside and started looking at books. Julia kept asking Gabriel what time it was. "Why don't you get a watch?" he finally said impatiently.

"I hate to wear watches."

"Yes, but you always want to know what time it is."

"OK, never mind, just tell me when it's four."

"Well, it's ten to four right now, so maybe we should go."

They hurried out the door and then Julia said, "Wait, the gloves." She ran back in and grabbed the leather gloves. They walked quickly down the ridge to the hollow where they'd seen the fawn.

Julia looked in first this time. "He's still there, and he's beginning to look restless."

"What should we do?"

"Let's go talk to my parents. If something has happened to his mother, he'll die if we leave him here."

They climbed back up the ridge to the cabin where they found Julia's parents still working in the garden. Julia told them about the fawn and Mother frowned. "It isn't like a doe to leave her fawn for that long. Maybe we'd better go look. What do you think, Jack?"

"OK by me. I could use a break anyway."

Julia's parents put down their shovels and the four of them walked back down the cliff. Julia led the way to the little hollow. Once more she separated the bushes and looked in and once more the same gentle eyes looked back at her. This time, however, the fawn didn't remain still. Something was clearly bothering him and he struggled to his feet as if he were expecting Julia to help him. His legs were so wobbly he could barely stand. Julia reached out her hand to steady him.

Mother was right behind Julia. She said, "Oh, look, Jack. He's so cute."

Father came closer and said, "Something must have happened to his mother. She would have come back by now."

"What can we do?" Julia asked in a pleading voice. "We can't just let him die."

"No, we can't just let him die," Father said. He bent down, picked up the little fawn and started back toward the cabin. "I can't climb the ridge while I'm carrying him," he said over his shoulder and he turned in the direction that led to the logging road. Mother followed him and Julia and Gabriel looked at each other in amazement.

"Well," Gabriel said. "I guess we have a fawn to take care of."

8.

Fawn

The next few hours were hectic. As soon as they reached the cabin with the fawn, Mother started helping Julia and Gabriel build a small pen beside the tool shed while Father drove into town to pick up a bottle and a nipple at the feed store. As he opened the door to the jeep, he said, "I'll see if I can find out something about the consistency of doe's milk while I'm there. I'd better hurry, though. It's almost four thirty."

Julia gathered some leaves and said, "I'll put them here beside the shed. He can lie down and we'll build the pen around him."

Mother led the fawn to the leaves and he lay there and watched as the posts went in and the wire was strung. Every now and then he gave a pitiful little bleat. Mother was just finishing the gate when Father returned. Fawn, as Julia and Gabriel had started calling him, was lying in the middle of the pen. As the jeep pulled up, Julia ran toward it and cried, "Father, did you get the bottle. He's so hungry."

Father got out of the jeep and handed Julia a glass bottle with a long black rubber nipple attached. "It's designed for lambs, but it should work for a fawn," he said. "The feed store owner knows the zoo keeper in the city, who's raised fawns in captivity before, so he called him and got the formula. It's much richer than cow's milk so we have to add fat—but no sugar. We must never feed him anything with sugar in it because it can upset the natural bacteria in his stomach."

Julia and Gabriel took the bottle and the bag of supplies into the cabin. They mixed together the formula which the feed store owner had written down on a piece of paper. Then they rushed outside and opened the gate to the pen. Julia held out the bottle and said, "Here, Fawn. We have some food for you."

Fawn raised his head and gave a little bleat. He grabbed the nipple with his mouth. He drank greedily. Father said, "I guess

63

he's so hungry, he doesn't mind the difference between the rubber nipple and his mother."

When Fawn finished eating, Julia and Gabriel sat down beside him and stroked his soft coat. Mother watched them for a few minutes and then said, "We have to be careful not to turn this fawn into a pet."

"Why?" asked Julia.

"Because it would be cruel. He would lead a lonely life—always following humans around. And he would be vulnerable to predators."

Julia sighed and said, "What do we have to do?"

"We'll keep him in the pen for a few weeks during the night, but in the daytime we need to make sure he's free to roam the woods. When he's a little bigger, he'll have to start sleeping in the woods, too. We'll feed him for now, of course, but when he's ready to be weaned, he'll have to eat what the other deer eat. And eventually, he must be free to return to his own kind."

Julia and Gabriel looked at each other and then at Fawn, who was lying sleepy and contented on his bed of leaves. "This won't be easy," Julia said to herself.

Gabriel stood up and said, "I'd better be getting back to the camp. It's almost dinner time. I'll come over tomorrow if that's OK."

Mother said, "Yes, I'm sure we'll need your help."

After dinner, Julia went back out to give Fawn another bottle. As she approached the pen, she looked in and saw that he was sleeping. His dainty forefeet were tucked underneath him and his head rested on the pile of dead leaves. As Julia walked in, he woke up and struggled to his feet. She held out the bottle. He drank eagerly and then settled back down into the leaves. Julia stroked his back for a few minutes and whispered, "Good night, little Fawn. I'll see you in the morning."

Fawn quickly became the center of Julia and Gabriel's lives. Gabriel came over every morning to help clean the pen. The first few days, they led Fawn through the gate of the pen as soon as the first bottle was finished. They quickly found they didn't have to lead him, however, because he followed them everywhere they went.

It was like having a baby. If Julia and Gabriel wanted to spend the day down at the meadow by the camp, they had to make Fawn's bottle first and put it in the back pack along with their sandwiches. "At least, we don't have to carry diapers," Julia said one morning as she put the long black nipple on the bottle.

Fawn loved going to the meadow. He ran from one end to the other, leaping gracefully over rocks and small hills. When he was tired, he returned and lay down beside Julia and Gabriel and watched the butterflies as they landed on the daisies and the Queen Anne's lace. On their way back to the cabin each day, Julia and Gabriel stopped along the logging road to show Fawn where he could find the leaves he would eventually eat. Each time they pointed to a leaf and touched it with their fingers, Fawn obliged them by taking a dainty little nibble.

When it was time for the late afternoon bottle, they took Fawn back to the pen so he could eat and then lie down for a nap. As they left the pen one day, Julia said, "How can we keep from turning him into a pet if he keeps following us?"

"I don't know," Gabriel said. "Maybe we should ask the tree."

"That's a good idea. We haven't been to see the tree since Fawn arrived."

Julia and Gabriel took the bottle back into the kitchen and washed it. Then they headed down the path toward the tree.

When they arrived, they both stood for a few minutes under his branches, gazing up at the newly opened leaves. Then they closed their eyes and gradually let their thoughts evaporate to make room for the voice of the tree. When he finally spoke, he went right to the point. "You want to know about the fawn."

Julia said silently, "Yes, how can we keep from turning him into a pet if he keeps following us?"

They stood and waited for the tree's response. When it came, it was with the sound of the breeze blowing through the rustling leaves. "He has to follow you now because he's an infant. But you cannot make him your pet."

"Why not?" asked Julia.

"Because he is to be your teacher."

"Our teacher?" said Gabriel out loud. Julia opened her eyes and looked at him. Then she shut them again quickly in case the tree had something more to say.

She heard nothing, however, except the singing of the birds and the tapping of a woodpecker. She opened her eyes again just as Gabriel opened his. "I guess that's it," she said.

"Yes, but what did he mean—our teacher? That little fawn?"

"I don't know. The tree is full of mysteries, isn't he? You're my brother, Fawn's our teacher and we have something important to do together. I suppose Fawn's part of that, too."

"Probably, but why doesn't he just explain himself?"

"Maybe because we wouldn't understand yet," Julia said.

"Yes, or maybe if we understood ahead of time, it would affect the way we do whatever it is we have to do."

Julia was silent for a moment and then she shivered in spite of the warm sunshine as another thought came to her mind. She looked at Gabriel with wide eyes and said, "Maybe, if we knew about it ahead of time, we wouldn't want to do it at all."

Gabriel said seriously, "Yes, I thought of that, too, but I didn't want to say it out loud."

After a couple of weeks, Mother said that Fawn needed to start sleeping outside the pen so one evening just before sunset, Julia and Gabriel took him into the woods, not far from the cabin. They made him a bed of leaves and waited until he lay down and closed his eyes. Then they left as quietly as they could so he wouldn't follow them.

That night Julia had a hard time sleeping. She imagined all sorts of disasters and had to stop herself from leaving the cabin in the middle of the night to go check on him. She knew her mother was right in insisting that he not be turned into a pet, but it was hard to know he was out there alone. At one point, she tried to contact him with her mind, but she couldn't concentrate. When morning came, she jumped out of bed and hurried to the door. Mother, who was fixing breakfast, said, "Where are you going?"

"To check on Fawn," Julia said over her shoulder as she opened the door. She jumped down off the step to the cabin and turned toward the path. Then she stopped abruptly—just before she tripped over Fawn, who was lying sound asleep right in the middle of the path. He had found his way back to the cabin during the night and had gone to sleep in the familiar place where he always waited for his bottle. Julia laughed out loud and he woke up. He struggled to his feet and bleated when he saw her so she went back inside to get the bottle.

As she prepared the formula, Julia told her mother what Fawn had done. Mother said, "Well, I guess you'll have to take him farther into the woods tonight."

So every evening for the rest of the week, Julia and Gabriel dutifully took Fawn into the woods and made him a little bed of dried leaves. And every evening he followed them back to the cabin and stood on the path by the door until Gabriel left for the camp and Julia went inside. Then he lay down right where he was and went to sleep. At the end of the week, Mother gave up and said, "Leave him alone. Maybe he'll figure it out for himself."

Fawn continued to sleep on the path for the next few weeks. Then in mid July, there was a rainy spell. It rained hard for almost a week. The first two nights, Fawn remained stubbornly on the path by the door. Each morning, Julia found him soaked and shivering. She brought towels to dry him off so he wouldn't catch cold. Then she led him back into the woods next to the cabin and explained that if he'd stay there under the trees, he wouldn't get so wet. Finally, by the third evening, when the rain started again, Fawn had had enough. On his own, he retreated into the woods and found the little nest Julia and Gabriel had made for him. After that, he went there every night even when the rain stopped.

Within a few weeks, Fawn had established a routine that would last for the rest of the summer. Each morning, he made his way out of the woods and stood patiently by the door until Julia appeared with his bottle. Then she went back into the cabin for her breakfast and Fawn amused himself by sampling the leaves from all of the trees and bushes that were in his reach, including the roses Mother had planted by the cabin. Fortunately, the vegetable garden was already enclosed by a tall chicken-wire fence and Mother quickly put a similar fence around the roses.

After breakfast, Gabriel appeared, carrying his lunch in a paper bag. Julia made herself a sandwich and the two of them set off to explore the woods with Fawn trailing along behind them. Julia and Gabriel brought their lunches and some water in a back pack, which they took turns carrying. They included a bottle for Fawn so that he could have his lunch when they had theirs. Even though Fawn was beginning to eat more from the forest, he wasn't ready to give up the bottle and continued to take it two or three times a day throughout the summer. Each afternoon around four, they returned from the woods and Gabriel went back to the camp. Julia then gave Fawn his last bottle after dinner and he went back to his nest in the woods.

Mother encouraged the trips through the woods. She said that Fawn needed to become familiar with his natural environment. One morning she said, "Why don't you and Gabriel take Fawn down to the deer run, the one that crosses the creek down in the valley of the forest."

So that morning Julia and Gabriel made their way carefully down the side of the ridge behind the cabin, past the pine grove where they had found Fawn and into the valley.

As they passed the pine grove, Julia said, "I wonder if he'll recognize the place where his mother left him."

"I don't know," Gabriel said. "Do you think he still remembers her?"

They watched as Fawn paused a moment and looked toward the grove and then hurried to keep up with Julia and Gabriel. Julia said, "I guess we've taken the place of his mother."

When they reached the creek, Fawn immediately went down to the water's edge and began to drink. Julia and Gabriel sat down on a rock and watched him until the mosquitoes started to whine around them. Then they stood up and continued their journey down the creek. As they turned to follow the path of the water around a large rock, they heard a rustle in the bushes and caught a glimpse of two adult deer, leaping over a fallen tree and fleeing into the forest.

Julia turned and looked at Fawn, wondering if he had seen the deer. He was standing still, gazing into the woods where they had disappeared. She said softly, "They're deer, like you, Fawn."

He glanced at her when she spoke and then with one graceful leap, he cleared the creek bed and vanished into the woods after the other deer.

"Fawn," Gabriel cried, "come back." He and Julia stood staring into the woods where Fawn had disappeared.

"Surely, he'll come back on his own," Julia said.

"But what if he can't find his way?"

"We'll stay here for a while and wait for him."

For the next hour, Julia and Gabriel stayed by the creek bed. They sat on the rocks and they waded in the creek. They ate their lunches and talked and waited, but Fawn did not reappear. Finally, they gave up and went back to the cabin. Julia's parents had gone to work on the fences so Julia and Gabriel had the cabin to themselves. They sat down at the kitchen table to discuss the situation.

"He's too young to make it on his own," Gabriel said. "He's not even off the bottle."

"I don't know what to do," Julia said.

They sat there for a few minutes, worrying, until Gabriel suddenly said, "I know. Let's ask the tree."

"The tree—of course. We've been so busy with Fawn we forgot about him again."

They hurried out of the cabin and down the path until they reached the old maple tree. Then they stood silently underneath his branches and closed their eyes. Together they sent out their appeal to the tree and then they waited impatiently for his answer. It came in the form of a scolding. "You're starting to forget," he said. "Don't get so busy that you lose sight of what's important."

"But isn't Fawn important?" asked Julia silently. "You said he was our teacher."

"A teacher can't teach if the student's mind is closed."

Julia thought about that for a moment and then said, "OK, I understand, but how do we get him back?"

"You don't understand or you wouldn't ask such a question."

"What do you mean?" asked Gabriel.

There was a pause and Julia and Gabriel heard the wind blow lightly through the leaves above their heads like a sigh. Julia felt that the tree was disappointed in her. She waited for his answer.

Finally the tree said, "If you want him back, you must contact him. Lead him home."

Julia thought about her experiences with the squirrels and the bird and then the one frustrating time she'd tried to communicate

with Fawn the night they first left him to sleep in the woods. She said, "I tried to contact him once, but I couldn't."

"That's because you were too attached. Your attachment made you worry. Worry is like a cloud. It covers up the sun and no light can come through. You have to let go and then he'll be there."

"OK," Julia said. "I think I really do understand this time."

She and Gabriel walked back to the cabin. Without a word, they both sat down on the step, right beside the place where Fawn always waited for his bottle. They closed their eyes. Julia explored her mind for tension and worry and slowly let it relax. She let the sounds of the forest gently lead her into the awareness of the moment with no thoughts of the past or the future and as she did, she saw the stream of light begin to appear. She let the light take her and she brought Gabriel's mind along with hers. He did not resist and they floated in a peace so deep that even the songs of the birds began to disappear. The light grew brighter and as they watched, it began to dissolve into a picture—a picture of the forest, dense and green with summer, and a small frightened fawn standing under a large tree.

Julia ignored the flickers of fear that were tugging at the edges of her mind as she gently reached out to Fawn. She spoke to him inside her mind the same way she spoke to the tree. "Here we are, Fawn," she said and she felt Gabriel's thoughts echoing her own. "Just follow the light and you can come home."

She saw Fawn turn toward her reaching mind and begin to walk. She and Gabriel sat there for over half an hour without moving. The mosquitoes came and they didn't notice. The singing of the birds grew louder as the afternoon wore on, but they heard nothing. They didn't move until they saw the image of Fawn climbing slowly up the ridge behind the cabin. Then they opened their eyes at the same time and walked silently to the edge of the ridge just in time to receive him as he came up over the crest. They looked at each other and smiled. Without speaking, they led Fawn back to the cabin and gave him the bottle that was still waiting in the back pack.

9.

Growing Up

One morning in mid August, Julia came out of the cabin to bring Fawn his bottle. He was waiting by the door as usual. Julia offered him the nipple and he started drinking. Generally, he finished the bottle quickly, but this time he stopped drinking half-way through. He started biting the nipple instead. Julia pulled the bottle back. "Fawn, what are you doing? You'll ruin the nipple."

Fawn nuzzled her arm with his nose and she held out the bottle again. He took a couple of swallows and then started biting. "No, Fawn." Julia pulled the bottle back. "What's wrong with you? Aren't you hungry? Are you sick?"

Julia looked at Fawn carefully. He didn't look sick. She said, "You stay right here. I'm going to go ask my mother what she thinks."

Julia went back inside. "Mother," she called.

Mother came out of her room. "What is it, Julia?"

"Fawn's acting strange. He took only half his bottle and then he started biting the nipple."

"Maybe he isn't hungry."

"Yes, but why? Is he sick?"

"Maybe he's been eating enough from the forest and doesn't need the bottle anymore."

"Hmm." Julia considered this possibility. "Could be. It's true he doesn't look sick. I'll go back and give him one more chance."

Julia picked up the bottle and opened the door. "OK, Fawn," she began and then stopped. Fawn wasn't standing by the door. Julia looked around. "Fawn," she called, "where are you?" She went down the path and looked around. "Fawn," she cried loudly. "Fawn, where are you?" She ran up to the pine grove where he slept, but he wasn't there. She looked around, expecting at any moment to hear him running through the ferns. But there was no sound except the calling of the birds. Fawn was gone.

Julia ran back to the cabin. "Mother, Mother," she cried. "Fawn's disappeared."

Mother came outside, carrying her gardening gloves. "What do you mean—disappeared?"

"He's gone. I can't find him anywhere."

"He probably just went for a walk in the woods." Mother didn't look worried.

"But he doesn't go into the woods alone—except to his bed in the pine grove—and he isn't there, either."

"Well, I'm sure he's all right. He's getting older, Julia. He can take care of himself now."

"He's not that old. His spots have only been gone a little while. I'm going to call Gabriel."

Julia went into the cabin and dialed Gabriel's number. When he answered, she said, "Gabriel, you have to come over right away. Fawn's disappeared."

"What? Disappeared where?"

"Well, if I knew, I could find him, couldn't I," Julia said impatiently. "He came for his bottle and then only took half of it. He started biting the nipple and I went in to ask my mom what she thought. When I went back out, he was gone."

"I'll be right over."

Julia put down the receiver. At least, Gabriel was taking this seriously. She felt irritated with her mother for her lack of concern. She paced back and forth across the kitchen floor a few times and then decided to walk down the path to meet Gabriel.

When Gabriel saw Julia coming, he called out to her, "Is he back yet?"

"No—what should we do? Do you think we could contact him?"

"We can try. Let's go to the place we were sitting when we first saw him."

Julia and Gabriel walked quickly back up the path. When they reached the fallen log by the grove where they had first found Fawn, they sat down and closed their eyes. Julia took a few deep breaths and tried to clear her mind, but she couldn't see anything except images of Fawn being pursued by coyotes or Fawn hopelessly lost in the woods. No matter how hard she tried, she couldn't find the clear beam of light that she knew would guide her to Fawn. Finally, she sighed and opened her eyes. "It's no use," she said. "I can't concentrate."

"Me either. I think we should go see the tree again."

Julia and Gabriel walked up the ridge to the cabin and continued down to the logging road. When they reached the tree, they closed their eyes and stood underneath his branches, waiting for him to speak. Finally, he said softly, "You're concerned."

"Fawn is gone," Julia said. She felt like crying.

"Fawn is fine. He's in the woods where he belongs."

"But will he come back?" Gabriel asked silently.

"From time to time. He's growing up now. He has to be more independent."

"You sound like my mother," Julia said scornfully.

"Your mother told you the truth."

"No, she didn't," Julia cried. "She doesn't care about Fawn. She's the one who sent him to sleep in the woods when he was just a baby."

The tree said sternly, "Julia, calm down."

"Calm down?" Julia's voice rose as she spoke. "Calm down? Fawn's lost in the woods and you want me to calm down?" She opened her eyes and saw Gabriel looking at her in amazement.

"Julia, you're arguing with the tree," he said.

"I don't care. He's just like my mother. He doesn't care about Fawn and he doesn't understand. I don't want to hear any more." Julia turned and started running up the logging road toward the cabin. Gabriel ran after her.

As they reached the cabin door, Gabriel said, "But, Julia, maybe he's right. Maybe your mother's right. Maybe Fawn is old enough to take care of himself in the woods. We said we wouldn't turn him into a pet."

"Whose side are you on anyway?" Julia opened the door to the cabin. Then she looked back at Gabriel and said angrily, "You don't understand, either. No one understands." She went inside, slamming the door behind her.

Mother, who was standing by the stove, looked up as Julia came in. "What's wrong?" she asked.

"Nothing."

"I heard you yelling at Gabriel."

"Gabriel's useless. Fawn's lost in the woods and nobody wants to do anything."

"But Julia ..." Mother put down her mixing spoon and started to say something else, but Julia went to her room, once again slamming the door behind her. She heard her mother open the cabin door and say something to Gabriel, who apparently was still waiting outside. Julia flung herself down on her bed and burst into tears.

That evening, when Mother came to her door to tell her dinner was ready, Julia said, "I'm not hungry."

"Don't you feel well?"

"No. I want to be alone."

Julia lay on her bed and stared at the ceiling. Where was Fawn? She knew he hadn't come back. Mother would have told her if he had. She closed her eyes and tried to contact him again, but it was no use. She was still too upset. Finally, she fell asleep. Her dreams were as agitated as her thoughts. In one of them, she was a young child again, sitting on the beach where she and her parents used to go in the summer. She was playing in the sand and watching the waves come in and go out. Each time the water retreated, she dug into the sand with both hands and closed her fists tightly. Then she watched as the water came back in and washed every grain of sand from her clenched fists. No matter how hard she held on, she couldn't keep the sand from slipping through her fingers.

She woke up crying. She thought about Fawn—how he'd follow her everywhere, how he'd nuzzle her arm when he wanted his bottle and how he'd lie beside her and let her stroke his soft coat. She thought about how cute he looked as he tasted the leaves in the forest and how much he'd loved her mother's roses before the fence went up around them.

"I'm losing him," she said to herself. "He's growing up and I'm losing him."

She lay awake thinking about the events of the day. She'd been angry with everyone. She'd even quarrelled with the tree. Maybe he'd never speak to her again. She'd snapped at Gabriel, too. All because they were trying to tell her something she didn't want to hear—that Fawn was growing up and didn't need her anymore.

The next day, even though Julia got up late, she still felt exhausted. She ate breakfast in silence. She knew Mother was watching her, wondering if she was all right, but she didn't have the energy to say anything.

After she washed the dishes, she went out and sat on the cabin steps. She knew she should call Gabriel and make up with him. She also knew she should go to the tree and apologize, but she was just too tired. Instead, she sat on the steps and stared out at the trees.

Mid morning, she heard the phone ring inside the cabin. A few minutes later, Mother opened the door and said, "It's Gabriel. He wants to know if he should come over."

"Tell him yes."

Julia was still sitting on the steps when Gabriel arrived. He sat down beside her without speaking. Finally, Julia said, "I'm sorry I yelled at you yesterday."

"That's OK," Gabriel said. "I know you were worried about Fawn." They sat in silence for a few moments and then Gabriel said, "Maybe we could try to contact him again."

"OK, let's try. We can go back to the log by the grove where we found him."

When they reached the place where they'd first seen Fawn, Julia walked over to the little grove and carefully pulled aside the blackberry bushes that were in the way. She looked down at that little hollow almost expecting to see him lying there, gazing at her with his big dark eyes. The hollow was empty, though, and Julia noticed that the ferns were growing high in the spot where Fawn once lay.

She went back to the log and sat down beside Gabriel. She closed her eyes and once again started the process of trying to clear her mind. This time it was easier. She let herself relax completely. She could feel the sun on her back. She could hear the buzzing of the flies. And she could see in her mind the faint glow of the beam of light that would lead her to Fawn if she allowed herself to follow it.

She wasn't sure how long they'd been sitting there when the images of the forest began to appear in her mind. She saw first the outline of a large pine tree. It shifted and wavered as she watched it and she wondered if it were being blown by the wind. Then she saw a ripple pass over its surface and she realized that she was looking at its reflection in the dark water of a little pool. She moved her gaze across the water and then she saw another reflection. She had the sudden impression of looking into a mirror, but it wasn't her own face she saw. Fascinated, she watched as the water rippled over the image of pointed ears and dark eyes— Fawn. She was looking at Fawn's reflection as he bent to drink from the pool. She was actually seeing through his eyes—the same way she'd seen through the eyes of the bird and the squirrel.

She continued to watch as he drank and then lifted his head and turned around. She found herself looking into the eyes of another deer, only slightly bigger than Fawn. She looked at the deer carefully and saw it was a female. So Fawn had found a friend—maybe even a future mate. Julia pulled her attention back quickly and opened her eyes.

Gabriel turned to look at her. "What is it?" he asked. "What did you see?"

"I feel like I've been spying on him." Julia stood up. "Did you see him?"

"No."

"Well, he's found a friend. He was with another deer."

"Then the tree was right. He is growing up."

"The tree—and my mother." Julia didn't like admitting that her mother had been right. "Gabriel, we're losing him. He doesn't need us anymore."

"Yes, I know. I wonder if this is how parents feel when their kids grow up and leave home."

"Maybe, but it happens gradually with people. With Fawn it's come so fast."

"Well, he may not be gone completely. He might keep coming for his bottle now and then."

"We'll see."

That evening at dinner, Julia made an effort to be cheerful with her parents, but she still felt sad inside. She didn't want to talk about Fawn but it was hard to think about anything else. Finally, she stopped talking and listened to her parents discuss the problems with the fences. Then Father got up, saying, "I made a fruit salad for dessert. I'll get it." He walked over to the counter and picked up the big blue bowl that was sitting there. He was turning around to come back to the table when he suddenly said, "What's that?"

"What?" Julia asked quickly.

"That noise."

Everyone was silent for a moment and then Julia heard it—the sound of something knocking against the cabin wall.

"Fawn," Julia cried and ran to the door.

It was Fawn, butting his head against the cabin wall. She went outside. "Oh, Fawn," she cried. "We missed you. I'll go get your bottle."

She went back inside. As she picked up the bottle, Mother said, "Here, Julia, I got you some rabbit pellets to feed Fawn if he came back. I think he's ready to give up the bottle."

"Are you sure?" Julia took a handful of the dry pellets. "They smell weird. What if he doesn't like them?"

"Try him and see."

So Julia went back to Fawn and held out her hand. He sniffed the pellets and then took them from her hand with dainty little bites. "Well, I guess my mom is right again. You don't need the bottle anymore." Julia stroked the outline of Fawn's baby spikes with the forefinger of her free hand. "I wonder what you'll look like with antlers," she said.

The next morning Fawn was still there. Julia gave him some more rabbit pellets, and he followed her down the path as she went to meet Gabriel.

Later that morning, Julia and Gabriel sat on a log in the pine grove by the cabin and watched Fawn as he browsed not far from them. Gabriel said, "He's stayed around for quite a while this morning. Maybe he didn't like being on his own."

"I don't know. I have a feeling he'll be going off again soon."

"Well, it's best that he's more independent. It would be cruel of us to try to hold him back."

"I know," Julia said, "but I'm going to miss him."

"Me, too. Maybe he'll still come visit us even when he's all grown up."

Julia watched Fawn take a few leaves from a small tree. "Will you, Fawn?" she called. "Will you come and visit us?"

Fawn turned his head at the sound of his name. He looked at Julia for several minutes and then went back to the leaves.

"Well," Gabriel asked, "what did he say?"

Julia sighed. "He didn't say yes and he didn't say no."

Julia and Gabriel had lunch inside the cabin that day with Julia's parents and Sam, who had come over to help with the fences again. Hunting season was only two months away and they wanted to have all the broken fences repaired before it started. When Julia and Gabriel went back outside, Fawn was gone.

10.

Secret Teachings

The last week of August, Julia and her parents went down to the camp to have lunch with Sam and Gabriel. After lunch, they sat outside, drinking hot apple cider.

"It's beginning to feel like fall," Sam said. "Look, all of us are wearing sweaters."

"Yes," Father said, "and some of the maples are starting to turn."

"School starts in a week," Mother added.

"Oh, no," Julia cried. "I was trying to forget about school."

"Don't you like school?" Gabriel asked.

"Well, it's OK, but I'd rather be outside."

"Actually, we do a lot of lessons outside. My dad's really into studying nature."

"I'd like that," Julia said. "Hey, I know what we could do. We could have school together."

"Oh," Gabriel said, "that would be great."

"Can we?" Julia turned to her mother.

"Well," Mother said, "what do you think, Jack, Sam?"

"I don't see why not," Sam said, "as long as they work hard and don't fool around."

"We won't fool around, will we Gabriel?"

"No," Gabriel said seriously. "I like to study and learn."

"Well," Mother said, "it would be more variety for both of them and they are in the same grade."

"Hurray!" Julia cried. Gabriel just smiled.

The next morning, Mother and Sam met at the cabin with Julia and Gabriel to work out the details for school. They decided to meet Monday, Wednesday, and Friday at the cabin and Tuesday and Thursday at the camp. Julia and Gabriel agreed that each school morning they would both leave their homes at 8:00 and meet halfway on the path they had made from the cabin to the camp. Then they would go to wherever school was being held that day. In the afternoon at 3:00, when school was over, they would reverse the process, walking together to the halfway point and then continuing to their homes alone.

They both had workbooks for math, English, and French grammar, which they would use every day. When they were with Sam, they would do science and natural history projects and when they were at the cabin, they would study literature and social studies with Mother and music, art and carpentry with Father.

Mother said, "I expect you're pretty much at the same level in most subjects."

"Except French," Gabriel said. "Julia's much better in French."

"That's because I've lived in Quebec all my life," Julia said. "But I can help you."

"I'm sure it will work out," Mother said. "Now for literature, which book should we start with?"

Gabriel said, "I don't know. What would you suggest?"

Mother made several suggestions, but each time she mentioned a book, either Julia or Gabriel had already read it. Finally, Gabriel said, "Well, we don't have to read the same book, do we?"

"No, I don't suppose you do," Mother answered.

Then Gabriel turned to Julia and said, "What was the best book you read last year?"

Julia thought for a moment and then answered, "I think my favourite was 'Nature' by Emerson. It isn't long because it's only an essay, but it takes a while to read because it isn't easy to understand. In fact, I thought it was too hard when I first looked at it, but Mother helped me and I ended up liking it the best of all the things I read."

"OK," Gabriel said. "Then that's what I'm going to read and we can discuss it together."

Julia's eyes brightened. "That's a great idea. Then I can enjoy it all over again. And what's your favourite book?"

Gabriel smiled and said, "I'll show you next week when you come to the camp."

"OK, I like surprises." Julia went to the book shelf to get her copy of *The Portable Emerson* and handed it to Gabriel. "The 'Nature' essay is here," she said, "on page seven."

The week-end before school started, Julia and Gabriel didn't see each other since both of them were needed at home to help chop and stack firewood. During the week-end Fawn came twice—once on Saturday morning and again on Monday, which was Labour Day. School was to start the next morning. Julia was glad to see Fawn and stopped her work immediately to feed him rabbit pellets and stroke his head. She realized, however, that the week before she'd been so busy thinking about school that she hadn't had time to miss him. She felt almost guilty as though she were somehow being disloyal or neglectful. As she watched Fawn trot back into the woods Monday evening, she realized that she was really looking forward to the first day of school so she could find out which book Gabriel had chosen for her.

The next morning was cool and clear—a perfect autumn day. Julia hummed one of the songs her father played on the flute as she walked down the path to meet Gabriel. When she saw him, she told him how she'd felt about Fawn the night before. "I don't understand why I should feel guilty," she said.

"I don't either. After all, we said from the beginning we wanted him to be independent."

"I guess people are strange sometimes."

"Yes, I guess so."

When they reached the camp, Sam was ready to do a science project, so Julia had to wait until late morning to talk to Gabriel about his favourite book. When they finally sat down at the table, after cleaning up the science equipment, Julia said, "OK, where's the book I'm going to read?"

Gabriel smiled and then went into his bedroom. He came back with a small book with a blue and gold cover and handed it to Julia. She looked at the title, which said *The Upanishads, Breath Of The Eternal.*

"Upanishad? What does that mean?"

"*The Upanishads* are part of the Vedas, which are scriptures from India." Gabriel paused and then said, "My mother gave me this book not long before she died. I didn't read it then, but she talked to me about it. I finally read it for the first time last year. I don't think I really understood everything, but it fascinates me."

Julia opened the book at random and read, "If the slayer think that he slays, if the slain think that he is slain, neither of them knows the truth. The Self slays not, nor is he slain."

"What does that mean?" Julia asked, "And why is the word 'Self' capitalized?"

"The Self is the part of us that is eternal—not the body or the mind—so it can't be killed, or slain, and it can't kill, either. At least, that's the way my mother described it."

"Is it like the soul then?"

"Yes, like the soul," said Gabriel. "Do you think you'll like reading this—or does it seem too strange?"

"No, it isn't too strange and yes, I think I'd like to read it. It reminds me of a poem I read by Emerson last year. It's called 'Brahma.' It's in that book I gave you. Give it to me and I'll show you."

Gabriel handed Julia the book. She opened it to the poetry section and flipped through the pages until she found the one she was looking for. Then she read:

If the red slayer think he slays,
Or if the slain think he is slain,
They know not well the subtle ways
I keep and pass and turn again.

"I liked the poem, but I didn't understand it very well when I read it last year. Maybe I will after I read this book."

"I'm sure you will because, if Emerson called his poem 'Brahma,' he must have read *The Upanishads*. They're all about Brahma—or Brahman, as it's written in my book."

"Is Brahman like God?"

"Yes, I'd say so," Gabriel said. "So, I'm reading Emerson and you're reading *The Upanishads* and we've already found a connection between the two of them. That's interesting."

"Yes," said Julia thoughtfully, "and you know what? I think there's a connection to Fawn, too."

"What do you mean?"

"I'm not quite sure yet, but I keep thinking about the tree saying that Fawn is our teacher."

"Yes?"

"Well, I don't know—it's just a hunch, but maybe these books are the words and Fawn is the experience."

"That's still vague, but I kind of see what you mean," Gabriel said. "You know, one of the definitions of the word 'Upanishad' is 'secret teaching.' I read it in the introduction to this book."

"Secret teaching—I like that," Julia said. "Yes, I think this book is just what we need right now."

That evening after dinner, Julia went to her room with *The Upanishads*. Instead of turning on the light, she lit a candle and placed it on the nightstand beside her bed. This book was too mysterious for bright electric lights. It needed the glow of candlelight.

Julia settled down on her bed and opened the book. She had to sit close to the candle so she could see the words. She felt as though she were sitting in a magic circle of golden light, surrounded by the shadows that flickered on the spruce-wood walls of her room. She skipped over the preface and the introduction until she came to the first section, which was called "Isha."

"I wonder what that means," Julia said to herself. The first page had a short summary of the section, which ended by saying, "The Self is Brahman and Brahman is all."

"There's that Self again," Julia said, "and Brahman—that means God. But does it mean that the Self is God?" Already the book was full of mystery.

Julia turned the page and read the first two sentences of the section, "In the heart of all things, of whatever there is in the universe, dwells the Lord. He alone is the reality."

Julia put down the book and thought about all the things in her world—the cabin, the trees, the animals—Fawn, wherever he might be in the forest. "So, the Lord—I suppose that means Brahman—is in all of them, too." Julia pondered this for a minute. "This sounds like something the tree would say."

Julia felt a twinge of guilt as she thought about the tree. She hadn't been to see him since the day she got so angry over Fawn. "I wonder if he's mad at me," she asked herself.

She picked up the book and finished reading the "Isha" section. Then she closed her eyes and thought about what she'd just read. "It keeps talking about the Self so that must be really important, but what is it exactly? I'll have to ask Gabriel about it again tomorrow."

The next morning, Julia woke up to another perfect autumn day. The sky was bright blue and the sun was shining on the maple leaves, which were already red at the top of the trees.

After breakfast, she hurried down the path to meet Gabriel. As she turned to walk with him back to the cabin, she said, "I read the first section. It keeps talking about the Self."

"I know."

"But what is it exactly?"

"The Self?"

"Yes."

"Well, my mother said it's who you really are."

"What?" Julia stopped and looked at Gabriel. "Say that again."

"It's who you really are."

"But that's amazing."

"Why?"

"Because the tree told me once I had to find out who I really am."

"He did? When?"

"Months ago—before I met you. I kept making up stories about my real identity—like I was a princess or a kid from another planet—but I knew that wasn't what he meant."

"Well, now you know," Gabriel said and started walking again toward the cabin.

"Yes, but I don't understand. I have a word for it—the Self—but I don't know what it means."

"Well, neither do I now that you mention it. Maybe we'll know more after you've been through the book."

"The tree said the understanding had to come from inside."

"*The Upanishads* talk a lot about the importance of meditation."

"They do? Like your mother told you to do?"

"Yes."

"Have you been doing it?"

"Not really—not since that one day. Have you?"

"Just once, but I think I'm going to try it again. It was pretty interesting."

"All right, I will, too," Gabriel said. "Maybe if we stick with it this time, we'll start to understand some of the tree's messages."

Julia said, "That would be nice for a change. So secret

teachings and meditation—this is definitely going to be an interesting school year."

11.

Lessons

As the school year progressed, Julia and Gabriel became more and more absorbed in the books they were reading. Every morning, as they did their math and grammar and French, they were both looking forward to the late afternoon when they could sit together and talk about what they had read the night before. They had this time to themselves. They read the books slowly, savouring every word. Sometimes, they couldn't read more than a page or even a paragraph at a time.

During the first weeks of October, Fawn came occasionally to the cabin, but his visits grew more and more infrequent. For Julia and Gabriel, however, as his physical presence became more rare, his presence in their thoughts and discussions increased. One day, as they were sitting at the table in Sam and Gabriel's kitchen, Julia said, "I don't see how you can keep from getting attached to an animal you take care of—and then, if you're attached, you want to have him around—and that's a kind of desire, isn't it?"

"Yes," Gabriel said, "I suppose it is."

"And, according to *The Upanishads*, you can't be free if you have desires."

"That's true, too," said Gabriel, "but the strange part for me is that, even though I know I did get attached to Fawn, I don't really mind not having him around all the time."

"I know," said Julia. "It's the same for me. I don't mind the reality of not having him around. It's just the idea of it I don't like."

"Hmm. Does that mean that what we get attached to is the idea and not the reality?"

One Saturday late in October, Fawn came again. Julia heard him scrape his horns against the cabin wall as she was finishing the dishes. She quickly dried the last cup and ran outside, grabbing the box of rabbit pellets on her way.

"Hello, Fawn," she said as she gave him a few pellets. "Gabriel will be here soon. Will you stay long enough to see him?"

Fawn ate the pellets carefully and nudged her arm for some more. Julia put one pellet in the palm of her hand. "Maybe if I give you only one at a time, you'll stick around longer."

Fawn was still there when Gabriel arrived. "Oh, Fawn," he cried, "how nice to see you." He stroked Fawn's head as Julia held out another pellet.

"Why are you giving him only one?"

"To make him stay longer."

"Maybe he'd come down to the meadow with us like he used to."

"That would be neat. Here, give him the pellets while I make my lunch."

Julia went into the cabin and quickly made a peanut butter sandwich. She grabbed an apple and another handful of pellets, which she placed in a plastic bag. Then she put everything in the pack and went back outside.

"Here, put your sandwich in." Julia held the back pack out to Gabriel.

"Just like old times," Gabriel said, "except we're packing rabbit pellets instead of a bottle."

Julia put the pack on her back and said, "Come on, Fawn. We're going to the meadow."

She and Gabriel started down the path and Fawn followed. When they reached the logging road, Fawn stopped and looked into the forest for a few minutes. Then he turned back to Julia and Gabriel.

"I guess he's decided to come with us," Gabriel said.

As they continued down the road, Fawn walked between them. When they approached the old maple tree, Gabriel said, "Do you want to stop?"

"To talk to the tree?"

"Yes."

"No, Fawn might get bored and run off."

"Have you visited the tree lately?"

"No."

"Why not?"

"I'm afraid he's mad at me for quarrelling with him that day."

"I think the tree's above being mad like that. It's too petty."

"You're probably right. Soon—I'll visit him soon."

When they reached the meadow, Fawn sniffed the golden rod and the Queen Anne's lace. Then he started grazing.

"He doesn't run and jump like he used to," Julia said.

"I guess he's more interested in eating."

"It's amazing that the grass is still so tall this late in the fall. Usually, we've had a hard frost by now."

When Julia and Gabriel ate their lunches, they offered Fawn some more pellets, but he wasn't hungry. He lay down in the grass beside them and went to sleep. Julia stroked his back while he slept. "He's changed, hasn't he?"

"That's inevitable," Gabriel said. "He's growing up."

"It's still nice to have him around, though."

The next morning, Fawn came again, and Julia and Gabriel once more took him down to the meadow. The weather was still warm for the end of October, but they could sense a change in the air. As they ate their sandwiches, the wind began to pick up and shift to the northwest. "Look at the clouds," Gabriel said, pointing toward the trees at the far edge of the meadow.

"Dark," Julia said. "And coming this way. It's going to rain soon, and it's getting colder."

"I guess we'd better go back."

"Yes, those clouds are moving fast."

Julia picked up the back pack and said, "Come on, Fawn." Fawn stood up and looked around with his ears raised. He followed as Julia and Gabriel walked quickly up the road.

The rain started just after they passed the maple tree. The wind blew even harder and the rain came pouring down. Gabriel cried, "Let's run for it. I'm freezing."

He and Julia started running up the logging road. Fawn followed them for a few minutes and then dashed off into the woods.

"Fawn," Julia cried.

"No, it's OK. He'll stay drier under the trees."

By the time Julia and Gabriel reached the cabin, they were soaked. Mother, who had been watching out the window for them, quickly opened the door. She held out two dry towels.

"You don't even have jackets," she said.

"It was so warm this morning." Julia was shivering so much she could hardly speak.

"Here, you've got to get on dry clothes. Gabriel can wear some of your sweat pants and a sweater." Mother went into Julia's room and came back with an armload of dry clothes.

"I'd better call my dad first," Gabriel said.

Julia took her clothes and the towel and went into the bathroom. "Take a hot shower," Mother called to her. "But make it quick so Gabriel can have one, too."

When they were warm and dry, Julia and Gabriel sat down with Mother to drink some hot tea.

"Where's Father?" Julia asked.

"Down at the camp," Mother said. "He's going to stay there until the wind and the rain let up."

"My dad said I should stay here," Gabriel said.

The rain didn't let up. It continued to pour all afternoon and the wind blew hard. Julia knew the cabin was safe from falling trees because of the cleared space around it, but it was dangerous to be out in the woods with the wind so strong. She hoped Fawn knew where to go.

Just before dinner, the power went out. Mother lit some candles and said, "I'm glad we have a wood cook stove." She put another log in and stirred the soup. "Gabriel, see if the phone still works. I think you'd better stay here tonight. I have a foam pad you can sleep on. And Jack had better stay at your place."

Just then the phone rang. Gabriel answered. "It's your dad," he said to Julia.

Mother took the phone. Julia heard her say, "That's exactly what I was just telling Gabriel. You stay where you are and I'll make a bed for him here."

After dinner, Mother got the foam pad and made Gabriel's bed on the floor of the kitchen. Then she sat by the stove with Julia and Gabriel and drank tea and told stories the way she used to when Julia was little. Most of these stories were about Mother's childhood and Julia knew them by heart. "Tell about the plays you and Aunt Celia used to do for Grandma and Grandpa," she said.

"Well," Mother said, and Julia settled back in the rocking chair as Mother told how she and her little sister had dressed up in old lace curtains and flowered straw hats and made up plays for their parents. They had pretended to be princesses or Christmas angels, and they'd made their dog play the part of the baby or the Thanksgiving turkey or Rudolph, the Red-Nosed Reindeer.

Julia watched Mother's face glowing in the candlelight as she spoke and laughed and gestured with her hands. "She's pretty," Julia told herself. "My mother's pretty. Maybe I will be, too, when I grow up." She brushed back her hair, which needed to be combed, and tried to imagine being a grown-up woman.

Mother finished her story and stood up. She stretched her arms above her head and said, "Bed time. Gabriel's yawning."

Julia got up and took the tea cups to the sink. As she walked toward her room, she said, "Good night, Mother. Good night, Gabriel."

Mother said, "Good night," and went into her room.

Gabriel said, "I hope Fawn's all right."

"Me, too."

That night, Julia lay awake for a few minutes listening to the wind and the rain. Then she fell into a deep sleep. She dreamed that Fawn had become small. She and Gabriel were wrapping him up in gauzy white curtains and carrying him around in the back pack. As they walked through the forest, it started raining and Fawn began to shrink, growing smaller and smaller until suddenly, he wasn't there at all.

The wind died during the night, and the rain settled down to a fine drizzle. Father came home after breakfast, bringing fresh clothes for Gabriel. Since it was Monday, Gabriel stayed at the cabin until school was over for the day.

The light rain continued off and on for days. The air was cold and the last of the leaves fell to the soggy ground. As the last weekend of October approached, Father became concerned about the fences again. "We have to finish them this weekend," he said one morning at breakfast. Everyone's going to have to work, rain or shine—even Julia and Gabriel. I'm going to hire Réjean as well."

"Well, let's hope the weather improves," Mother said.

The weather didn't improve. Saturday morning it was still cold and wet. Sam, Gabriel and Réjean came up from the camp after breakfast. Julia and her parents got in the jeep and followed Sam's truck up the logging road to the fence line.

"The road's getting muddy," Father said. "A couple more days of this rain and the jeep won't make it through in places."

Repairing the fences was miserable work. Mother and Father put in the new posts. Sam and Réjean strung the barbed wire with the fence puller, and Julia and Gabriel came along behind to hammer in the staples. Julia felt grouchy all day. She was cold and wet and her hands were scratched from the barbed wire in spite of the leather gloves she was wearing. Everyone worked silently except Réjean, who hummed softly to himself. Julia was irritated by his humming. She didn't want anyone to be cheerful when she felt so awful. Only the thought that repairing the fences might protect Fawn and the other deer from the hunters kept her going. She knew that hunting season started the following weekend.

Throughout the next week, Julia continued to worry about Fawn. In spite of the new fences, she dreaded the beginning of hunting season. She'd always hated the sound of gunshots and this year, knowing Fawn was out there somewhere made her tremble with fear. "I hope at least he has the sense to stay on the property," she told herself.

The week of hunting season, the sun returned, but the weather remained cold. Julia tried to concentrate on her studies and ignore the sound of gunshots. Once, in the middle of a science experiment, Gabriel looked up and said, "It's hard to tell where the shots are coming from with all the echoes."

"I know," Julia said. "I just hope they're outside the property."

"Well, at least the fences are fixed."

After school on Friday, Julia walked half-way down the path with Gabriel. As she turned to go back to the cabin, she heard another gunshot ring out. She walked slowly, her head down. Her mind was troubled and turbulent. The sun was gone again and the sky was heavy with clouds. Most of the leaves had fallen. The trees no longer sparkled with colour. Only the beech trees held on to some of their leaves, which wouldn't fall until the new buds opened in the spring. The air was chilly and Julia knew that a cold rain, or possibly snow, was on the way.

As she climbed the ridge up to the cabin, Julia thought about Emerson saying that nature reflected the emotions of people. As she looked at the dark branches of a tree against the grey sky, she thought, "Well, if that's the case, I must be in a really bad mood." She shrugged her shoulders as if she were trying to shake off the gathering gloom and opened the door to the cabin.

As Julia walked into the kitchen, she knew instantly that something was wrong. Father was standing at the window, looking out into the woods. Mother was in front of the stove, stirring something in a large pot. Her jaw looked tight and she had an angry expression in her eyes.

"What's wrong?" Julia asked.

Mother looked up and tried to smile.

"What's wrong?" Julia repeated.

Mother put down the spoon. She walked over to the table and sat down. "Someone shot a deer inside the property."

"What?" Julia cried. "But the fences have been fixed."

Father turned from the window. "They cut the wire and came in—right in front of a No Hunting sign."

"How did you find out?" Julia asked.

"We heard the shots. They seemed too close to be outside the property so we went up to investigate. We saw two men from the jeep as they were dragging the deer through the broken fence. We got out, but the brush was too thick and we heard their vehicle drive off before we could get there."

"Did you see their car?"

"No," Father replied. "It sounded more like a truck than a car, but that's all we know."

Julia sat down beside Mother. She said softly, "Then Fawn is in danger."

Mother said, "No, they aren't supposed to shoot deer that young."

"They aren't supposed to cut the fence either."

Her parents didn't reply. Julia stood up and went into her room. She put her books on the desk and sat down on the bed. She closed her eyes and tried to contact Fawn, but she couldn't make her mind be still. She sat there until she felt a couple of tears slip through her closed eyelids. Then she said silently, "Please, God, Brahman, whoever you are. Please take care of him. He's so little." She allowed herself a few more tears and she felt some of her anxiety begin to dissolve. As her mind became quiet, she caught a fleeting glimpse of a tawny body, leaping over a fallen log. "Take care of yourself, Fawn," she whispered. "I don't want you to get shot." Then she thought about *The Upanishads* and the immortal, shining Self that can't be killed and she added, "But you are free."

12.

The Trial

Julia woke up the next morning to the sound of icy rain hitting sharply against her window. She was glad it was Saturday. She didn't feel like walking down the path to meet Gabriel. In fact, she didn't feel like doing anything—not even getting dressed and going out to eat breakfast. She lay in bed for a while, listening to the rain, and then finally, she sat up and reached for *The Upanishads*, which were on the nightstand beside her bed. She opened the book at random, as she had the first time she saw it, and read:

> *This universe is a tree eternally existing,*
> *its root aloft, its branches spread below.*
> *The pure root of the tree is Brahman, the immortal,*
> *in whom the three worlds have their being,*
> *whom none can transcend, who is verily the Self.*

> *The whole universe came forth from Brahman,*
> *moves in Brahman, mighty and awful is he,*
> *like to a thunderbolt crashing loud through the heavens.*
> *For those who attain him death has no terror.*

Julia raised her eyes from the book and looked out the window. The rain was coming down hard now, striking against her window like icy needles. She could see the dark forms of the leafless trees through the misty air and the heavy clouds rolling in the turbulent sky. She sighed and closed her eyes focusing her attention on the sound of the rain. It seemed to be speaking to her, but she wasn't sure she wanted to hear what it was saying. She had the impression of a coming trial, like the image of Brahman, mighty and awful, crashing through the heavens like a thunderbolt. She felt a shiver of fear run through her body.

She sat for some time with her eyes closed. She watched in fascination as the sound of the rain began to form an image in her mind—the image of a tree, the old maple, whom she had not visited since the day of the argument. She saw him standing steady and majestic, as always, and then, as the wind gave a sudden gust outside her window, she saw his bare branches move ever so slightly, as though he were beckoning her to come to him. She waited to see if he would speak, but he remained silent so she finally opened her eyes and got out of bed.

The rain stopped during breakfast, but the air remained cool and a dense fog settled on the forest. When she finished the dishes, Julia put on her coat and walked slowly down the path. As she turned onto the logging road, she heard another gunshot. She shuddered. "How can they see what they're shooting at in this fog?" she asked herself. She started walking faster toward the old maple tree. The fog was so thick she could see only the outline of the tree looming above the road. As she approached, she was startled to see the shadowy shape of a man move out from behind the broad trunk of the maple. Julia stopped, her heart beating fast. "Who's there?" she said softly.

The man walked toward her. "Julia?" he said in a deep voice.

Julia watched as a face with dark eyes and a grey mustache emerged from the fog. "Réjean?" she said in amazement. "What are you doing here?"

Réjean stood silent for a moment, as if considering her question, before he answered. "Visiting," he said.

"The tree?"

Réjean looked back at the maple and said thoughtfully, "An old soul." Then he looked at Julia and said, "I'll be going back to the camp now. Take care."

Julia watched as he disappeared quickly down the road. She stood gazing into the fog and then slowly walked toward the tree. She placed her hands on the rough, wet bark and closed her eyes. "You called me?"

The tree responded at once. "Yes, you have much to do. It is almost time and you must be strong."

"It involves Fawn, doesn't it?"

There was a pause and then the tree replied, "Yes," and once again he said, "You must be strong."

Julia waited for a few moments, but heard nothing except the rustling of dead leaves as a slight wind stirred them from their resting places on the ground.

As soon as she got back to the cabin, Julia called Gabriel. "I've been to see the tree," she told him.

"What did he say?"

"Can you come over?"

"Well, I'm in the middle of ..."

Julia interrupted. "It's important."

"OK, I'll be right there."

By the time Gabriel arrived, the wind had picked up and was blowing the fog away. The sun shone weakly through the clouds. Julia met him on the path and told him what the tree had said.

"I wonder if we could contact Fawn," Gabriel said.

"I don't know. I've been trying, but I haven't had much luck."

"Well, let's try again. Let's go back to the log down by the grove where we first found him."

"OK." Julia opened the door to the cabin where her mother was sweeping the kitchen floor. "Gabriel and I are going for a walk."

"That's fine," Mother said, "but don't go too far from the cabin. We've fixed the fence, but there's no guarantee it won't be cut again. Any place too close to the fence line could be dangerous."

"All right," Julia said. She and Gabriel left the cabin and started down the ridge to the pine grove where they'd first discovered Fawn. When they reached the log they had sat on that day, Julia paused and looked toward the bushes at the edge of the grove. Then she shook her head and sat down on the log beside Gabriel.

Without a word, they closed their eyes and began trying to clear their minds. It was difficult, but they persisted. They both knew it was important that they succeed in contacting Fawn. Julia focused her attention on the sounds of the forest—the twittering of chickadees, the calling of crows, the wind and the mysterious stirring of small animals in the bushes.

Julia became aware of Gabriel's mind as hers began to settle down. Their two minds together made one beam of energy, reaching through the forest, searching for Fawn. Julia could see this energy passing through the trees and the bushes. Each detail was clear, from the dead leaves lying on the ground to the graceful arch of the ferns, now rust-coloured from the cold autumn wind. Their minds passed like a search light through a tangled snarl of blackberry bushes to a large rock shaped like a rounded pyramid and then around behind the rock to a soft bed of leaves where Fawn lay silently watching and listening to the forest. Julia let her mind rest on him lovingly for a moment. She felt she could almost reach out and touch his elegant body. She gazed at his gentle eyes and his pointed ears, alert to the tiniest sound of danger, and as she watched him, she slowly became aware of what lay behind him, not more than two feet away.

Julia gasped. She opened her eyes and turned to Gabriel. "What is it?" he said, startled.

Julia stood up. "The fence—he's right beside the fence. Did you see it?"

Gabriel stood up, too. "You're right," he said. "We have to go get him."

"But will he stay there until we find him?"

"I don't know, but we have to try. Let's go."

They hurried up the ridge, careful to bypass the cabin at a safe distance. They knew they were disobeying Julia's mother, but they didn't have time to explain. Julia could feel her heart beating hard as they reached the old logging road and started to run. As they ran, the wind blew hard against their backs and sent the dry leaves on the road flying before the steady motion of their feet.

They ran for almost twenty minutes and Julia felt her breath become heavier and heavier until she thought she couldn't continue. Then suddenly, she felt herself being lifted above her breath and carried by it as though her body had become as light as a falling leaf. She felt that she could run forever.

Julia knew the logging road well, and as they came to a turn which had been made to go around a large pine tree, she called to Gabriel, "We're almost there."

He nodded and they continued as the road came to a small hill. As they reached the crest, Julia stopped abruptly. Gabriel stopped, too, and turned to look at her. She pointed down the road and he turned back to look in the direction of her finger.

"I see," he said, "it's the fence line."

She nodded and said, "Now what?"

Gabriel started to answer but just then a shot rang out, shattering the peace of the forest. Julia looked at Gabriel in alarm as a second shot was fired. "That was close."

"Come on," Gabriel said, "this way." He leaped off of the road and into the woods. Julia followed him as he made his way through the underbrush. She tried to be as quiet as possible, but she could hear the crunch of the dead leaves with every step she took. She saw that Gabriel was moving with purpose. She knew that something was pulling him and she followed him as if she were in a dream.

She saw him struggle through some blackberry bushes. She saw him emerge into a little clearing and she saw him walk up to the large rock, shaped like a rounded pyramid, and look around him. And then she saw him fall to his knees and she heard him cry out, "No—no—not again."

As she walked up to stand behind him, she looked up at the sky and saw in her mind the image of a small boy, sitting up in his bed, alone at night, listening to his father crying in the next room. Then she allowed herself to look down at Gabriel. He was leaning over the body of their Fawn, and she knew that Fawn was dead.

Time seemed to stand still as Julia stood there watching. Gabriel was crying bitterly, but Julia still felt as though she were in a dream. "This can't be real," she thought. "This just can't be real."

She moved closer to Gabriel and put her hand gently on his shoulder and, as she did so, she heard a soft voice say,

"Gabriel, Gabriel." She looked up and there beside the rock stood a woman, dressed in a white robe. She had long black hair, straight like Gabriel's. She was looking at him with such love that it brought tears to Julia's eyes.

Gabriel was still bent over Fawn. Julia saw the woman gently lift her hand and a ray of light went from her fingers to Gabriel. As her hand slowly rose through the air, his head also lifted. He looked at the woman for a moment and then said softly, "Mother? You've come? And I see you. Are you real?"

The woman smiled and looked at Julia and said, "Your sister sees me also."

Gabriel turned to Julia and she nodded. Then he looked back at his mother and said, "Why did Fawn have to die?"

The woman smiled again and said, "There is no death, Gabriel. You know that. The spirit of Fawn no longer needs to be in the body of an animal. It is ready to move on. But there is another who is not ready—who still has much to learn—and he needs you now."

"Another?" Gabriel said, looking around at the forest.

"Yes, there were two shots—remember?"

"Yes," Gabriel said, "but where?"

"Look in the brush to your left. You will see him."

Julia walked over to the bushes to Gabriel's left. As she approached, she heard a low moan, as if someone were in pain. She parted the bushes with her hands and then she saw him— a young man, a boy really, not many years older than herself and Gabriel. She said, "Gabriel, come here."

Gabriel came and stood beside her as they looked at the boy. He was lying on the ground. His face was pale and his breathing was shallow. There was blood on his shoulder and a gun lying on the ground beside him. Julia turned back to Gabriel's mother and spoke to her directly. "Who is he? And what happened? Did he shoot Fawn?"

"No, the man who was with him fired both shots. He didn't know what he was shooting at. He saw movement in the bushes and he was hasty."

"Where is he now—the other man?" asked Gabriel, his face looking suddenly dark with anger. "He has to be punished."

His mother said gently, "No talk of punishment now, Gabriel. He isn't far from here, but he's hiding because he can hear the sound of our voices and he's frightened. You must call him. You need his help to get the boy out."

"Call the man who shot Fawn?" said Gabriel in disbelief.

"Yes," said his mother. "You must call him, and there's something else you must do."

"What's that?" Julia asked.

The woman looked at her and then back at Gabriel and said, "You must forgive him."

"Forgive him?" Gabriel cried. "Forgive the man who killed our Fawn?"

"Gabriel, you're forgetting again. Look at me. There is no death. But you'll never know that is true—not for Fawn, not for me and not for yourself—unless you can forgive."

Gabriel was silent for a moment. Then he looked at Julia with a question in his eyes. Julia returned his gaze and said, "Yes, Gabriel. It's hard for me, too, but I know she's right."

Then she watched as Gabriel's face slowly began to soften and he started to cry again. He looked back at his mother and said, "I thought I'd lost so much when you left, I couldn't stand the thought of losing anything else."

His mother said gently, "Nothing is ever lost, Gabriel. I'm still here."

"Yes, you are," he said. "OK, I forgive him. Now, how do I call him?"

"You're only forgiving him with words right now, but it's a start. Later, you'll forgive him with your heart. You can call him Jim. That's his name."

Julia and Gabriel together turned toward the fence and called loudly, "Jim, Jim, come here. We need you."

When they turned back toward the rock, the image of Gabriel's mother was gone, but they could still feel her presence strongly. They stood in silence for a moment until they heard a rustling in the bushes. Then they watched as a man carrying a gun slowly made his way through the underbrush into the clearing where they stood.

13.

Jim

The man named Jim stopped abruptly when he saw Julia and Gabriel. He looked at them and then down at Fawn, who was lying at their feet. "Oh," he stammered, "Oh, no, he's only a fawn." Then he looked at Julia and Gabriel again. He saw the sorrow in their eyes and said, "Was he your pet? I don't know what to say."

Gabriel answered tensely, "He was our friend, but we'll talk about that later. There's another problem."

"Another problem?"

"Yes, you shot twice."

"But I missed the first time."

"You missed the fawn," Julia said. "Come here," and she led Jim to the bushes where the boy lay.

She looked up at Jim as she parted the bushes with her hands, and she saw his face turn white as he realized what he was looking at. "Stevie?" he gasped. "But—but—I sent you to the truck." Then he looked at Julia with bewildered eyes. "I sent him to the truck," he repeated.

"Evidently, he didn't go."

Jim turned and knelt beside the boy. Julia could see his hands shaking and she knew he was in shock.

"He's still alive," she said, "and we need your help to get him out of here."

"Yes, OK," Jim said. "Yes—a doctor—the hospital. We have to take him to the hospital."

The thought of concrete action helped Jim focus his mind. He set down his gun. Then he put his hands gently under the boy's back and raised his head onto his lap. The boy moaned and Julia could see the hole in his shirt where the bullet had passed through his shoulder. The wound bled a little when he was moved.

"Easy does it, Stevie," Jim said. "You're going to be all

right. We're going to take you to the hospital." Then he looked
at Julia and said, "Do you think that you and your friend could
carry his legs?"

"Yes, of course," Julia said. Gabriel came forward and each
of them picked up one of the boy's legs. Together they lifted
him as gently as they could and started carrying him toward the
road. Julia tried to walk carefully, but the ground was uneven,
and she could see that every movement was causing the boy
pain. His face was white and he moaned from time to time, but
he didn't open his eyes.

When they finally reached the road, they stopped for a
moment and Gabriel said, "It's going to be a long walk down
to the cabin."

Julia started to answer and then paused. "No, it isn't—listen, I hear the jeep."

Gabriel turned his head toward the road and said, "You're
right. I hear it, too. It's coming this way. Let's walk to meet
them."

They started out again, but they hadn't gone far when they
saw the jeep come around a bend in the road, followed by Sam's
truck. "It looks like everyone's come," Julia said. "I guess they
were worried about us."

They stopped walking and let the jeep approach. Father
was driving and he pulled up in front of them. Mother was sitting in the passenger's seat. They both opened their doors and
got out. They were followed quickly by Sam, who had parked
his truck beside the jeep. "Julia, thank God you're all right. We
heard shots. What in the world has happened?" Mother cried.

"This boy has been shot and we have to get him to the hospital quickly. Can you drive us?" Then she turned to her father
and said softly, "Father, Fawn's been shot, too. He's dead. He's
back by the pyramid rock, close to the fence line. Could you
get him? I want him to have a funeral."

Father looked at Mother and said, "I guess the explana-
tions will have to wait. Irene, can you drive them to the hospital while Sam and I get the fawn?" Then he turned back to Julia
and said, "When things settle down, Julia, we're going to have
a long talk."

"Yes, I know," Julia said. "I'll tell you everything. Or at least, I'll try."

Then Father looked over at Jim, who still hadn't spoken. "I expect you have some explaining to do, too, mister."

"Yes, sir," Jim said. "I do—as soon as the boy's taken care of."

Julia, Gabriel and Jim held on to Stevie and moved out of the road so Mother could turn the jeep around. Then Jim and Gabriel got in the back seat with Stevie between them, leaning against Jim's shoulder. Julia sat in front with her mother, who started driving down the old logging road. No one spoke as they drove through the woods. They passed the path to the cabin and then the old maple tree. Julia glanced at him as they drove by and wondered what he would have to say when she finally had a chance to talk to him. Mother drove as quickly as possible, but the road was rough and difficult in places. Finally, they passed the entrance to the campground and a few moments later, they emerged from the forest onto the road which led to town.

Everyone breathed a sigh of relief. The ride was smoother now and the hospital was only about fifteen minutes away. Julia

glanced at Gabriel in the back seat. She could see that his jaw
was tight and he was looking intently out the window at the
passing countryside. Julia knew that he hadn't really forgiven
Jim and she knew that she hadn't either. The thought of Fawn
lying dead in the forest was like a hard little knot inside her
mind. She wanted to let go of it, but she didn't know how. She
looked at the face of the boy. He was still pale and his breathing was shallow. Then she slowly turned her attention to Jim.
He was looking down at Stevie. He had one arm around his
shoulder and the other arm against his waist to steady him so
he wouldn't fall over. She saw both tenderness and anguish in
Jim's face and she felt her heart begin to soften a little. Then, as
she watched, she saw one small tear escape from beneath his
lowered eyelid behind his glasses and slowly trace its way down
his cheek. "Is he your son?" she asked.

Jim looked up. "No, my nephew—but he's like a son to
me. I don't have any children of my own. He's my sister's boy.
Her husband died when Stevie was only four and I've tried to
fill in as a father. If he were to die ..." He choked back a sob
and a few more tears escaped.

"He won't die," said Julia, as she remembered what
Gabriel's mother had said.

Jim looked at her, astonished by the authority in her voice.
"How do you know?" he asked.

"Because he still has too much to learn in this lifetime."

As she spoke, she could feel Gabriel looking at her, but she
kept her eyes on Jim's face. He stared at her for a few seconds
and then looked back at the boy. "Well, I only hope you're
right," he said.

Julia said, "I know I'm right."

Mother said, "We're here," as she turned the jeep into the
hospital parking lot and drove to the entrance marked
"Urgence."

She stopped the jeep and said, "Stay here. I'll go get someone." No one spoke as she got out of the jeep and walked
quickly through the emergency room door. Julia could feel the
tension in the jeep. Everyone's eyes were fixed on the entrance

to the emergency room. They didn't have long to wait. Less than five minutes after she had disappeared through the door, Mother re-emerged with three young men in green, who were carrying a stretcher. They opened the door to the jeep and told Jim to get out. He gently lowered Stevie's head to the seat of the jeep as he backed out of the door. Then one of the young men reached in and eased the boy out and onto the stretcher, which was held by the other two. They carried Stevie into the hospital with Jim and Mother walking ahead of them. Julia and Gabriel followed along behind.

Once they were inside the door, things happened fast. Stevie was placed on a bed with wheels and rolled down the hall, where he disappeared behind two large swinging doors. Julia saw a sign that said, "Chirurgie," over the doors. "They're taking him to surgery," she whispered to Gabriel. Jim and Mother went over to the reception desk to answer questions. Julia could hear Jim telling the story of the accident in shaky French and she saw that her mother was listening intently. She heard the woman behind the desk ask about Stevie's parents. Jim explained that his father was dead and his mother had gone to Montreal for the day with Jim's wife and wouldn't be back until late evening.

Julia looked around the waiting room, which was practically full. There were several families with young children, who were coughing or leaning feverishly against their parents. There was a middle aged man with a bandage over one eye and a woman sitting with her ankle up on a chair. These were the less serious cases, who were at the emergency room only because the regular clinics were closed for the week-end. Julia could see that many of these people were also trying to listen to Jim's story and she realized that Stevie's entrance had provided some excitement.

Finally, Julia heard the woman behind the desk explain to Jim that the hospital had to inform the Sûreté Québec about all accidents involving firearms. She saw Jim nod his head and reach up to push his glasses back as they slipped down his nose. Then the woman made a phone call. A few moments later, a police officer came in and took Jim into a corner where he could talk to him privately. At one point, the policeman returned to the reception desk and beckoned to Mother.

Julia watched her walk over to the desk and then she turned to Gabriel and whispered, "I forgot to tell you something."

"What?" Gabriel whispered back.

"When I went to see the tree this morning, someone was already there."

"Who?"

"Réjean."

"Réjean?" Gabriel spoke out loud.

"Shh." Julia held her finger against her lips.

"What was he doing there?" Gabriel whispered.

"He said he was visiting."

"Visiting the tree?"

"I guess so. He said something else, too—he said, 'An old soul.'"

"About the tree?"

"I think so. But isn't that a weird thing to say? I mean, I know the tree's old, but ..." Julia paused.

"Well, Réjean is pretty weird. Not that he isn't nice. He helps people a lot—sometimes they don't even know. But he's so secretive. He just stays in the background, like a shadow."

"Yes, that's exactly how he seemed—like a shadow, appearing out of the fog. It was actually pretty creepy."

"As for the old soul remark," Gabriel continued, "my mother said something like that once. She said that people who are very evolved are old souls because they've had a lot of incarnations to grow and learn in."

"But the tree isn't a person."

"Yes, but he is evolved. He's very wise."

"Why would an evolved soul come back as a tree?"

"I don't know. He must have his reasons." Gabriel looked toward the reception desk. "Look the policeman's talking to your mother now," he said.

Julia turned around. She could see that the policeman was asking a question and she saw her mother shake her head.

When Mother came back to sit beside her, Julia said, "What did he ask you?"

"He asked if we were going to press charges for trespassing, and I said no." She paused and looked at Gabriel and said, "I think the poor man has enough to deal with."

Julia nodded and looked at Gabriel to see if he agreed, but he only stared at the floor and said nothing.

Finally, the policeman was done. Jim came back and sat down in a chair facing Julia. She could see the heads of the other people in the waiting room turn as Jim walked by. Everyone was curious about the presence of the policeman. She heard one little boy say to his mother, "Mommy, what did that man do? Is he a bad man?"

His mother leaned over and said, "Shh, be quiet, Daniel."

Julia looked at Jim. She could see that he was still shaken. She said, "Are you in trouble with the police?"

Mother said, "Julia!"

Jim shook his head and said, "That's OK. Your daughter has a right to know what's going on." Then he turned back to Julia and said, "No, I don't think so. Your mother was kind enough not to press charges and I think the officer believed that it really was an accident about Stevie. I just have my own conscience to deal with."

Julia could tell that Gabriel was listening intently even though he was still staring at the floor. Jim continued, "If Stevie just recovers, I'll be eternally grateful, but I don't know how I can make it up to you two—I mean, about your fawn, you know."

Jim paused. Suddenly, Gabriel raised his head. He looked directly at him and said, "Why did you shoot Fawn?"

Jim sighed. He pushed his glasses up his nose again and said, "Well, you see, I'm the president of our hunters' club. I used to be a really good shot, but something happened in the last few years and I haven't been able to hit anything. I had pretty much given up for the day and I'd sent Stevie back to the truck. I was going back myself when I saw the fawn move through the leaves of some bushes. I didn't really see the fence, but I did know it was close. Anyway, I guess my pride was at stake and I didn't want to go back to the hunters' club and tell them that I hadn't gotten anything again this year because today is the end of the season. So I just shot without bothering

to see that the deer was too young. And then I saw him moving so I knew I'd missed and I shot again. And you know the
rest." Jim looked down at his boots and Julia saw his glasses slip
down his nose again.

Gabriel said, "So what are you going to do now?"

Jim looked back at Gabriel, but before he could speak,
Julia saw one of the emergency room doctors walking toward
them. She said, "There's the doctor."

Jim stood up as the doctor approached and said, "The boy
is out of surgery. You may come see him now."

14.

Stevie

As Jim started to follow the doctor, Julia stood up, too. Mother said, "No, Julia, only Jim can go see him right now."

Julia started to sit back down, but Jim turned to her mother and said, "No, that's all right. She can come—and Gabriel, too, if he likes. After all, they did save his life."

Julia looked at Gabriel and nodded and he stood up, too. As they crossed the crowded waiting room, Julia was again aware of the attention of the other people sitting there, but she didn't look at them. She and Gabriel followed Jim and the doctor down the hall to a room with a closed door. The sign on the door said "Salle de Reveille." "What does that mean?" Gabriel asked.

"Waking Up Room," Julia answered.

The doctor slowly opened the door and Jim went in with Julia and Gabriel behind him. There were four beds in the room, each separated from the others by a big curtain, which hung on a metal rod and could be pulled open and closed. The doctor walked to the bed in the far corner and pulled the curtain open a little. Julia could hear the large metal rings of the curtain scrape against the rod. She and Gabriel walked over to the corner and stood just inside the curtain as Jim walked up to the head of the bed where Stevie lay. His face still looked pale. Julia could see that his left shoulder and arm were covered with a large bandage.

The doctor said, "He should be coming out of the anesthetic any minute now. You can talk to him, if you like." Then she pointed to a long cord that was hanging by the bed and said, "Just pull this cord if you need anything and a nurse will come." Jim nodded and the doctor left the room.

Then Jim leaned his head toward Stevie and said softly, "Stevie, can you wake up now?" Julia held her breath as she watched Stevie's face. At first, she saw no movement, but then, slowly she saw his eyelids flicker. Jim leaned close again and said, "Stevie, Stevie." He put his hand on the boy's head.

Stevie's eyelids fluttered again and then opened slightly. He moved his head as though he were looking for something and then he said, "Where's the fawn?"

Jim didn't answer and the boy said again, "Where's the fawn?" Then his eyes opened wider. He looked around the little cubicle and then up at Jim. Julia knew that he had just realized he was no longer in the woods. "Uncle Jim," he said. "Where am I? What happened?"

Jim sighed and said, "It's a long story, Stevie. There was an accident and you were shot—and so was the fawn. It was my fault."

Stevie's eyes opened wide and he said, "You shot the fawn? Oh no, Uncle Jim. He wasn't even wild. He just stood there looking at me. When I reached out my hand to him, he even came toward me. He was so beautiful."

"Yes, Stevie, I know," said Jim. "I made a terrible mistake." He shook his head and said again, "A terrible mistake."

Stevie closed his eyes a moment and then opened them and looked straight at his uncle. "I can't do it anymore," he said. "I can't go hunting with you anymore, Uncle Jim. I never really wanted to hunt anyway. I only went because I wanted to be with you."

"I know, Stevie, I know," said Jim. "I think I always knew you didn't want to hunt. But you don't have to worry. I'm not going hunting anymore either. I'm through."

Julia felt Gabriel move slightly as Jim spoke. "You?" Stevie exclaimed. "But you're the president of the hunters' club."

"Well, I'll just have to resign. It's finished. I know that for sure."

There was a pause and Julia turned to look at Gabriel. His eyes were fixed on Jim's face and Julia could tell that he was moved by Jim's vow to give up hunting. She could feel Gabriel's tension and mistrust beginning to melt away like the ice on the creek in the springtime.

Julia cleared her throat and Stevie looked at her as if he had just noticed that she and Gabriel were in the room. Jim beckoned

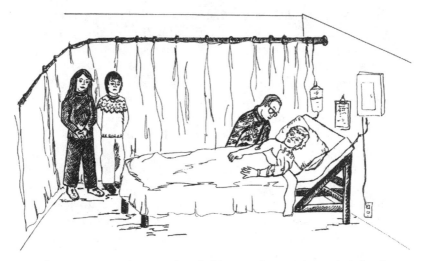

them to come closer and said, "Stevie, this is Julia and Gabriel. They saved your life. The fawn belonged to them."

Julia said, "He didn't really belong to us. We raised him to be free. He belonged to himself and to nature —but he was our friend."

Stevie said, "He was so beautiful. You must be very sad."

Gabriel said, "Yes, we are." Then he looked at Jim and said, "Did you mean it when you said you were giving up hunting?"

"Yes," Jim said. "I certainly did."

"And will you explain to your hunters' club what happened?"

Jim's face flushed and he swallowed hard. "That would be difficult, but if you think it would help, then yes, I will."

Gabriel looked at Jim intently a moment as if he were searching every corner of his mind and then he said, "OK, in that case, the death of Fawn will not have been for nothing."

"Yes, I guess that's true." Jim looked at Julia and back at Gabriel and said, "Maybe, you two could come with me. You might have something to say to the hunters, too."

Julia and Gabriel looked at each other and nodded. Gabriel said, "OK, we will," and he smiled.

There was a moment of silence and then Jim said, "Well, Stevie, I think we'd better let you rest now. When your mom gets home, I'll bring her here to see you."

Stevie nodded. Julia and Gabriel said good bye and promised to return. Then they walked with Jim back to the waiting
room to find Julia's mother.

When they left the hospital, the sky was already dark. Jim said,
"You don't have to take me to my truck. I'll get somebody to
drive me up there tomorrow. My place is on the way. You can
just drop me off there." Mother nodded and they all got back
in the jeep.

On the way to Jim's house, nobody said anything except
for Jim giving directions. Julia realized that she had a lot to
think about. She knew that once they left Jim at his place,
that could be the end of the relationship with him and Stevie,
but somehow she didn't think that would be right. She felt
like something had been started that wasn't finished yet—and
anyway, she and Gabriel had promised to visit Stevie again
and go to the hunters' club meeting with Jim.

When they pulled into Jim's driveway, the house was still
dark. Jim said, "I guess my wife and sister aren't back from
Montreal yet." Julia could tell that he was not looking forward
to sitting in that house alone, waiting to tell them what had
happened to Stevie. She felt a sudden rush of sympathy and
almost wished that she and Gabriel could stay and wait with
him. On an impulse, she said, "Jim, do you want to come to
Fawn's funeral tomorrow?"

Everyone looked at her in astonishment and Jim said, "Oh,
I don't want to intrude on your family like that."

Julia said, "It wouldn't be an intrusion. Funerals are supposed to be for everyone who's grieving." She paused and
looked at Gabriel, who was sitting in the back seat of the jeep.
She could see his dark eyes staring at her, reflecting the light of
a street lamp beside Jim's driveway. He was obviously surprised,
but he didn't seem displeased. She looked back at Jim and said,
"And you are grieving about Fawn, aren't you?"

"Yes, Julia, I am." Then Jim turned to Mother and said,
"What do you think? Would it be all right with you and your
husband if I came?"

Mother glanced at Julia and said, "Yes, it would be all

right. I think I understand what Julia means. It might be a kind
of healing."

Julia said, "OK, then it's settled. How about one in the
afternoon?" Mother nodded and Julia added, "And maybe
afterwards, we could visit Stevie again."

After they left Jim, Mother drove as quickly as possible to the
camp ground to take Gabriel home. She and Julia said good
night to Sam, who came out to the jeep to greet them. Mother said that Gabriel could explain everything that had happened at the hospital. Julia could tell that she was tired and just
wanted to get home.

During the drive to the cabin, Julia kept waiting for
Mother to start asking questions, but she didn't say anything.
As they drove past the old maple tree, Julia could feel his presence, solid and reassuring, but also challenging, there in the
silence of the dark woods. She made up her mind to go visit
him first thing in the morning.

When they arrived at the cabin, Father had dinner waiting
for them. Julia suddenly realized how hungry and tired she was.
She hadn't eaten since breakfast. The air was chilly and her
father had built a fire in the cook stove. The cabin was cozy and
welcoming after such a long, difficult day. As they came in the
front door, Julia said, "Father, did you get Fawn?"

"Yes, we did, and we dug a grave for him, too—right in the
woods there where he used to sleep."

"Thank you," Julia said, and she hugged her father.

During dinner, Julia and her mother talked about their trip
to the hospital and Stevie's operation. Then Father said, "We
found their guns in the woods and brought them back. They're
in Sam's truck. I guess we'll have to return them."

Julia said, "We can give them back, but they won't be
needing them. They've both given up hunting for good," and
she told her parents about the visit that was planned to the
hunters' club.

Father said, "Well, I'm not too surprised, considering all
that's happened. It does show that Jim has a conscience, though."

"He does have a conscience," Julia said. "He's actually a

good person. He loves Stevie very much, that's for sure." Then she said, "He's coming to the funeral tomorrow. I invited him and Mother said it was all right."

Father looked surprised, but then he said, "Well, it seems a little strange, but I guess everything's a bit strange about this whole adventure." He looked over at Mother and back at Julia. "We haven't forgotten that you have some explaining to do," he added.

"I know," Julia said, "but couldn't it wait until tomorrow, when Gabriel and Sam are here?"

"Yes," Mother said. "I think we're all too tired tonight anyway. Maybe they could come over in the morning and then stay and have lunch with us."

"OK," Father said. "We'll call them in the morning. Now, let's clean up the kitchen and go to bed."

It didn't take long to clean the kitchen and Julia was glad to go to her bedroom, where she could be alone with her thoughts. As she got into bed, she said a little prayer for Fawn. Then she pulled the covers up around her shoulders. As she lay there in the darkness, she expected to feel sad about Fawn. She felt like she needed to get her mourning out of the way and she was prepared for a good cry. As she closed her eyes, however, she found she couldn't even picture the body of Fawn, lying in the woods. Instead, all she could see was a shining white light, which surrounded the image of a beautiful woman with long, black hair, who smiled and said, "Don't you remember? There is no death."

15.

The Funeral

The next morning the air was still cold, but the sun was shining brightly. Julia got up early. She ate breakfast and washed the dishes as quickly as she could. Then she said to Mother, "I'm going for a walk." She left the cabin and headed down the path in the direction of the old maple tree. The air was still and the leaves that clung to the branches of the beech trees shone like copper in the sunshine.

When Julia reached the tree, she walked under his branches and sank down gratefully into the cushion of leaves that covered the ground. She leaned her head against his trunk and closed her eyes. She sat there a moment, resting in the comfort of being near the tree again. She had so many things to ask him, she didn't know where to begin so she let the first question rise to the top of her mind by itself. She breathed deeply and said silently, "What am I going to tell them this morning? How can I explain everything?"

The tree answered almost immediately, "Tell them the truth."

"But where do I begin?"

"At the beginning, of course."

Julia said, "You make it sound so simple. What if they don't believe me?"

"They will believe you because it is simple. There isn't anything that you've done that they couldn't do also if they could simply clear their minds—and on some level, they already know this."

"I see," said Julia. "Well, I'll give it a try because I don't really have any other choice."

She sat silently for a moment and tried to plan what she would say to Sam and her parents, but the tree interrupted her thoughts. "Don't plan," he said. "It's better to wait for the inspiration of the moment."

Julia sighed and said, "OK, I'll try." Then she added, "In that case, I have another question. How can Fawn be our teacher when he isn't even around anymore? What are we supposed to be learning from him?"

"If you think he isn't around anymore, then you probably haven't learned it yet."

"What do you mean?"

"What did Gabriel's mother tell you?"

Julia sat up straight and opened her eyes. She looked up at the branches of the tree. "You mean, you know Gabriel's mother?" she said out loud.

There was a moment of silence and Julia quickly shut her eyes again, but she continued to sit up straight. She had the distinct impression that the tree was laughing. She couldn't hear anything—not even in her mind—but she could feel waves of merriment flow through her and she could almost see his branches dancing in the cool sunny air.

The tree repeated his question, "What did Gabriel's mother tell you?"

Julia answered, "She said that there is no death."

"Do you believe that?"

'Well, I don't really understand what she means. It's true that we were able to see her and talk to her, but she isn't around all the time in Sam and Gabriel's lives like she used to be. And we haven't seen Fawn. He just isn't here anymore. I can't pet him or feed him rabbit pellets. He just isn't here." Julia felt sad and angry when she thought about Fawn. She said, "You have to admit there has been a change."

"Yes, on the physical level there's been a change."

"But I don't really know any other level," Julia cried. "I see things. I feel things. Even when I turned into the bird, I could see the nest and feel the eggs. That's what's real to me—what I can see and hear and feel."

The tree was silent for a moment, and Julia thought he was done. She started to stand up, but then she thought she heard him sigh. She leaned back against his trunk and closed her eyes.

"Remember the seeds, Julia," he said softly.

"What seeds?" Julia waited, but this time there was no answer.

Julia arrived at the cabin just as Sam's truck pulled up. Sam and Gabriel got out and Sam went into the cabin to find Julia's parents. Gabriel stayed outside to talk to Julia for a few minutes. His face was tense and Julia knew that he didn't feel prepared for the meeting. As soon as Sam had shut the cabin door, Gabriel said in a low voice, "Did you go see the tree?"

"Yes."

"Good, what did he say?"

"He said to start at the beginning and tell the truth."

"Even about my mother?"

"About everything," Julia replied and then added, "He seems to know your mother."

"Really? What did he say?"

"Well, he asked me if I remembered what your mother had told us."

"What did you say?"

"I was surprised and I said, 'Do you know Gabriel's mother?'"

"What did he say then?"

"He just laughed."

"Laughed? What does it sound like when a tree laughs?"

"It doesn't sound like anything. You can just feel it."

"Amazing—so is that all?"

"No," Julia said, "We talked about death not being real and I told him I didn't understand. Then he told me to remember the seeds."

"What seeds?"

"I have no idea. He wouldn't tell me anything else. You know how he is."

"Right. He takes you to a certain point and then leaves you there to think about it."

"Yes, well I guess I'll have to think about seeds—as soon as we get this meeting out of the way." Julia paused and looked toward the cabin. She said, "I think we'd better go in now."

"OK," Gabriel said and reluctantly followed her through the cabin door.

Julia and Gabriel walked into the kitchen and sat down at the table. Mother poured them each a cup of tea. Julia took a sip and said, "OK, what do you want to know?"

Mother looked at Father and Sam and said, "Well, to begin with, why were you up in the woods with Fawn when we told you to stay close to the cabin?"

"Because we knew that Fawn was in danger," Julia replied.

"How did you know he was in danger?" Father asked.

"Because we could see him and he was lying too close to the fence."

"I don't understand. How could you see him? Where were you?"

"We were down on a log behind the cabin," said Gabriel. "The same place that we were when we found him."

"But how could you see him from there?" Sam asked.

"We could see him in our minds," Julia said. "The same way I saw the fire at the camp ground—remember? And the squirrel that was up in the ceiling?"

"Do you mean that you have psychic powers?" Mother asked.

"I don't know about any powers," Julia answered. "I only know that we can see things if we really focus our attention. The tree says ..." Julia stopped. She wasn't sure that she really wanted to talk about the tree—especially after she saw the way her mother was looking at her.

"The tree?" Father said. "What tree?"

Julia sighed and continued, "The old maple tree beside the road. He talks to us sometimes."

"Talks to you?" Sam said. "Out loud?"

"No, not out loud—in our minds," Gabriel said.

"Then it's just your imagination," Mother said.

"Maybe," Julia said, "at least, I used to think so—except that Gabriel hears the same things I do."

"So—you started to tell us what the tree said," Father reminded her.

"Yes, well, the tree says that everyone has the ability to see things—that people just need to clear their minds and focus their attention."

Julia's parents looked at each other and then at Sam. Their

faces were grim. Finally Mother said, "I can't hide the fact that
this concerns me a great deal. It's not that I don't believe in psychic powers. It's just that I'm not sure they're healthy—especially for young people, whose minds are still immature."

Julia didn't say anything so Mother continued. "I think
that Sam and your father and I need some time to consider
this. It's almost lunchtime and then Jim will be coming for
Fawn's funeral. Then I think you and Gabriel are planning to
go with him to the hospital to visit Stevie. Is that right?"

"Yes," Julia said.

"All right," Mother said. "Then let's eat now and perhaps
we can continue our discussion when you get home."

"All right." Julia got up to help set the table. As she took
the plates out of the cupboard, she had the sinking feeling that
things weren't going the way the tree had said they would.

Everyone was silent during lunch. As soon as cleanup was
over, Julia and Gabriel went outside for a few moments before
Jim arrived for the funeral. They walked over to the woods to
look at the grave, which Sam and Father had dug. There was
a cushion of dead leaves at the bottom and Fawn's body was
already lying there. Julia and Gabriel looked at him for a
moment, and Julia said, "He looks like he's just sleeping."

Gabriel nodded and then he said, "Julia, what are we going
to do about our parents? They don't seem to understand."

"I know. The tree said they would, but maybe he didn't
mean immediately. Right now, though, we just have to focus
our attention on Fawn's funeral."

"That's true. I brought the Emerson book. I thought I
could read the poem about Brahman."

"I guess I knew you would," Julia said. "I'm going to read
the section from *The Upanishads* that that poem is based on.
Also, my parents are going to play music at the beginning and
we're all going to sing 'Amazing Grace' at the end."

"My dad carved a little wooden statue of Fawn. It's mount-
ed on a spike so we can put it in the ground to mark the grave."

"That's nice." They stood for a moment looking at Fawn,
lying so still on his bed of leaves, and then they closed their eyes

and tried to clear their minds. They stood silently beside the grave until they heard Jim's truck pull into the parking area in front of the cabin. Then they came out of the woods, greeted Jim, and went to get their books for the funeral.

A few moments later, they all gathered solemnly around the grave. Father had his flute and Mother had her guitar. They began playing a song that Father had composed. Its melody floated sadly and sweetly in the cool November air. When the music was over, Gabriel opened the Emerson book and read:

If the red slayer think he slays,
Or if the slain think he is slain,
They know not well the subtle ways
I keep, and pass, and turn again.

Far or forgot to me is near;
Shadow and sunlight are the same;
The vanished gods to me appear;
And one to me are shame and fame.

They reckon ill who leave me out;
When me they fly, I am the wings;
I am the doubter and the doubt,
And I the hymn the Brahmin sings.

The strong gods pine for my abode,
And pine in vain the sacred Seven;
But thou, meek lover of the good!
Find me, and turn thy back on heaven.

Julia listened with her eyes closed. When Gabriel was done, she opened *The Upanishads* and read:

The Self, whose symbol is OM, is the omniscient Lord.
He is not born. He does not die. He is neither cause nor
effect. This Ancient One is unborn, eternal, imperish-
able; though the body be destroyed, he is not killed.

*If the slayer think that he slays, if the slain think that he
is slain, neither of them knows the truth. The Self slays
not, nor is he slain.*

*Smaller than the smallest, greater than the greatest, this
Self forever dwells within the hearts of all.*

When she finished, everyone was quiet for a moment, and then
Julia said, "We haven't asked Jim if he wanted to say anything."
    Jim looked at her, startled, and then he said, "Well, I did-
n't plan anything, but maybe the twenty-third Psalm would be

appropriate." Julia nodded. She bowed her head and closed her eyes. Jim's voice sounded shaky as he began:

The Lord is my shepherd, I shall not want.

As he continued, his voice became gradually stronger and deeper and Julia thought that he sounded like a minister she had heard on the radio once. She listened intently as the beautiful words of the psalm filled the woods like music:

He maketh me to lie down in green pastures.
He leadeth me beside the still waters.
He restoreth my soul.
He leadeth me in the paths of righteousness
for His name's sake.
Yea, though I walk through the valley
of the shadow of death,
I will fear no evil for Thou art with me.
Thy rod and Thy staff, they comfort me.
Thou preparest a table before me
in the presence of mine enemies.
Thou anointest my head with oil.
My cup runneth over.
Surely, goodness and mercy shall follow me
all the days of my life
And I will dwell in the house of the Lord forever.

When Jim finished, no one spoke. Julia could hear the air still ringing with the sound of his voice. Then Sam cleared his throat and took a handful of dry leaves. He dropped them into the grave on top of Fawn's body. Everyone else picked up some leaves and did the same. When Fawn was completely covered with leaves, Father took his shovel and filled the rest of the space in with earth. Then Sam took the deer he had carved and thrust the wooden spike into the earth on top of the grave. Julia gathered another handful of dry leaves and spread them around the little carving as her parents picked up their instruments.

Finally, everyone sang "Amazing Grace." Julia could hear her own voice high and thin in the midst of the others, and she felt as though she were watching from a distance. When the last note died away, everyone turned and walked out of the trees into the clearing by the cabin. Then Julia and Gabriel followed Jim to his truck and the three of them left for the hospital.

16.

Mira

Even before they walked into Stevie's room, Julia knew that he was much better because she could hear him laughing. This time, she didn't wait for Jim. She just opened the door and walked in. Stevie was sitting up in bed, talking to a woman, who looked a lot like Jim. As Julia entered, the woman looked at her and pushed her glasses up on her nose. Another woman was sitting at the foot of the bed. She had straight dark brown hair, mixed with grey, and a sweet smile. Julia smiled at the women and then looked over at Stevie. He was smiling, too, and she noticed that his eyes were bright blue, just like hers. His face was no longer pale and his blond hair shone in the sunlight, which streamed through the window beside his bed.

"Julia, how nice—and Gabriel, too," he said. "How good of you to come see me."

"You look much better," Julia said.

"I feel much better. I'm going home tomorrow. Julia, Gabriel, I'd like for you to meet my mother and my aunt Stella, Jim's wife."

"Mary Thomas," the woman sitting closest to Stevie said as she stood up to shake hands with Julia and Gabriel. "You can call me Mary. My brother has told me what you did for Stevie. I can't begin to thank you enough."

"Nor can I," Stella added. "And for my husband as well. You've been very kind."

"There's no need to thank us. Our reward is that we've made a new friend—two new friends," Julia said, looking back at Jim.

"Well," Mary said. "I hope that we'll make the third and the fourth." She smiled at Stella, who nodded and smiled back.

Julia said, "That sounds good to me."

The nurse came in just then, bringing chairs. As soon as everyone was settled, Gabriel asked Stevie how old he was and

131

where he went to school. Stevie said, "I go to the high school here in town. I'm sixteen," he added. "And you?"

"We're both fourteen," Julia said. "And we go to school at home."

"Really?" Mary said. "How does that work?"

Julia and Gabriel proceeded to explain their school situation. Then Stevie talked about his school and how he liked singing in the choir and studying literature and natural sciences. The time passed quickly. Finally, Jim looked at his watch and said, "It's almost supper time. I'd better be getting you two home."

Gabriel said, "OK, but when are we going to the hunters' club?"

Jim said, "How about next week? Stevie wants to go, too. He should be strong enough by then. Give me your phone numbers and I'll call you as soon as I've made the arrangements."

Gabriel wrote out the phone numbers. Then he and Julia said good bye to Stevie and Mary and Stella and left with Jim. In the truck on the way back, they continued to chat with Jim, but Julia had a funny feeling in her stomach as they got closer to the cabin and the meeting with her parents and Sam.

As they got out of the truck and said good bye to Jim, Gabriel whispered to Julia, "I'm nervous."

She whispered back, "I am, too, but the tree says it will be all right—eventually."

Julia and Gabriel went into the cabin and found their parents waiting with dinner already on the table. They all ate in silence and washed the dishes quickly.

Then they sat back down at the table and looked at each other warily. Finally, Father said, "Julia, Gabriel, we feel that this has gotten out of hand and as parents, we have to do something about it. That old maple tree seems to be the source of the trouble and, as a matter of fact, we were talking about cutting it down, even before any of this happened."

"Cutting it down?" Julia gasped. "Why?"

Mother said, "It's old and part of the trunk is beginning to decay. It's taking up space that younger trees could use and we don't want it to blow over in a wind storm."

"But—you can't do that!" Julia cried. "That would be worse than what Jim did to Fawn. At least, that was an accident. This would be cold-blooded murder."

"Julia," Mother said. "Calm down. It's just a tree."

"Just a tree? Just a tree? You're wrong! You don't understand!" Julia was so angry and upset she could hardly speak. She leaned forward, her elbows propped on the table, searching for the right words to somehow make her parents see the horrible consequences of what they were suggesting. "You—you—" she grasped for words, but her mind was whirling in confusion and frustration.

Suddenly, she saw Gabriel sit up straight and she could hear the tension in his voice as he said, "And what are you going to do about my mother?"

"Your mother?" Sam said.

Julia turned to look at Gabriel. He was staring at Sam with a cold glint in his dark eyes. "Yes, my mother," he said. "What are you going to do about her. You can't cut her down with your chainsaw."

Julia saw the colour drain from Sam's face as he said, "What do you mean, Gabriel?"

134 *Julia*

"She talks to us, too—just like the tree. We even saw her. She was there the day Fawn was shot."

Sam stood up slowly. "Gabriel," he said in a controlled voice. "This has gone too far. You've let your imagination carry you away. Something has to be done—and right away. Now, come with me. We're going home." For a moment, Gabriel didn't move. Sam raised his voice a little and said, "Gabriel—now."

Gabriel stood up and moved to the front door like a sleep walker. Julia and her parents sat motionless as they heard Sam and Gabriel get into the truck and drive away. Then Julia stood up and, without a word to her parents, walked into her room and shut the door.

Julia didn't sleep much that night. She tried to communicate with the mind of the tree, but she was too upset to focus her attention. She spent most of the night tossing and turning in her bed, rehearsing angry speeches, addressed to Sam and her parents—speeches which she knew she would never deliver and which only aggravated her anger and frustration.

The next morning she didn't come out of her room until it was almost time for school. Neither of her parents were in the kitchen so she ate a few bites of cereal, washed the breakfast dishes and sat down at the table. She looked out the window, watching for Gabriel, since she'd gotten up too late to go meet him halfway. He arrived a few minutes late and Julia could tell from the way he walked up the path that he'd had a bad night, too.

He came in and sat down at the table across from Julia and said, "Hi." Mother came out from her bedroom, carrying her notebook. She tried to smile and said, "Hello," but Julia could tell that she was forcing herself to be cheerful. Julia and Gabriel looked at her but did not respond. She handed them a sheet of paper with their lessons for the day and asked them if they had any questions. Julia shook her head and her mother said, "All right. I have some things to attend to. You may work on your own this morning," and she went out the door.

As soon as she left, Gabriel said, "Well, did they say anything else last night?"

Julia shook her head again and said, "No, I just went to my room. How about your dad?"

"The same. I could tell that he was not in the mood to listen to reason and anyway, I was too mad to be reasonable. We didn't talk on the way back to the camp and I went straight to bed when we got there. We didn't really speak this morning either, but I have the feeling he's planning something."

"Like cutting down the tree?"

"Yes, like cutting down the tree. It really bothered him when I mentioned my mother."

"I could see that. So what are we going to do? We've got to stop him."

"I don't know. I imagine he'll try to do it while we're in school."

"Well, we'll hear his truck if he drives up—and we'll certainly hear the chain saw."

"Right—but then what?"

"I have no idea," Julia said, "no idea at all." She paused and then said, "Gabriel, is it possible that the tree was wrong? That we shouldn't have told them the truth?"

"I don't know. I didn't think the tree could be wrong, but it doesn't seem to be working out very well."

For the rest of the morning, they tried to do their lessons, but they both found it hard to concentrate. At lunch-time, Julia's parents came in and joined them. They tried to make conversation, but Julia and Gabriel didn't say much. Toward the end of the meal, Mother said, "Julia, you've hardly eaten."

"I'm not hungry," Julia replied.

"Well," Father said. "Would you like to do some music this afternoon?"

"Not really," Julia said.

"All right," Mother said. "Then you can continue with your math workbooks after you've cleaned up the kitchen."

"Fine." Julia felt relieved when her parents went outside again.

Julia and Gabriel cleared up the lunch dishes and then got out their math books and sat back down at the table. They worked in silence, but Julia knew that neither of them was concentrating on math. They were listening for the sound of Sam's truck coming from the camp ground to the tree. Julia looked out the window where her parents were splitting and stacking wood. She saw them stop every so often and look out into the trees in the direction of the road and she knew that they were listening, too.

Finally, around two, they heard it. Julia had been musing over an algebra equation when she suddenly became aware of a low rumbling sound in the distance. She looked at Gabriel. He said, "That's him, I'm sure."

"Let's go." They grabbed their jackets and headed for the cabin door. They ran down the path toward the road. Julia heard her parents calling her and then running after them, but she paid no attention. She had only one thought—to save the old maple tree.

They reached the tree just as Sam was bending over his chainsaw, ready to pull the starter cord. Gabriel screamed, "No, Daddy, no—you can't!" and rushed toward Sam.

Sam cried, "Gabriel, stay back." Mother and Father came running up, and Mother grabbed Julia's arms. As Julia struggled to free herself, she saw her father take hold of Gabriel, who was trying to get to Sam. She heard Father say, "No, Gabriel, the chainsaw's too dangerous. You have to stay back."

Julia cried, "Let me go," and tried to pull away, but Mother only tightened her grasp. Sam pulled the cord to the chainsaw, which sputtered, but didn't start. For a moment, Julia had a frantic hope that he wouldn't be able to get it started, but he pulled the cord again hard, and the chainsaw began to roar like a wild animal. Just then, Gabriel broke away from Father and started running toward Sam again.

Julia shouted, "Gabriel, be careful," but before he could reach his father, Gabriel tripped on a tree root and fell to his knees in the soft cushion of dried leaves that covered the ground. She saw him look up helplessly as Sam started toward the tree and then she heard his voice—loud and piercing—rising above the roar of the chainsaw, crying, "Mother—Mother—do something!"

And then everything seemed to happen in slow motion. The echo of Gabriel's voice hung suspended in the air and the roar of the chainsaw suddenly stopped as though the motor had died. Julia saw Sam put the saw on the ground and bend over it, preparing to pull the cord again. Then she saw the air in front of the tree begin to shimmer as though the beams of sunlight coming through its branches were shifting, and an image began to form—the image of a woman in a long white robe, with shining black hair and dark eyes. She heard Mother gasp and felt her loosen her grip on Julia's arms. She heard Father say, "What in the world?" and then she heard the voice of Gabriel's mother—the voice which had echoed in Julia's mind like music ever since the day Fawn died—saying, "Sam, dear, leave the saw alone. It isn't going to run today."

Gabriel, still kneeling on the ground, lifted his arms toward his mother, who raised her hand. The light which surrounded her seemed to extend until it touched Gabriel's hands and his whole body began to glow. Sam dropped his chainsaw and Julia heard him say, "Mira? My God, is it really you?"

Gabriel's mother said, "Yes, Sam, it is. You should listen to Gabriel. He only tells the truth." Then she pointed to the tree. Waves of light shimmered and flowed from her hand to the trunk of the tree, and the tree began to glow, too. She said, "You can't kill the tree, Sam, even if you cut him down and burn the wood. His spirit is immortal and will simply take another form—just like the spirit of the fawn. No," she repeated, "you can't kill the tree, but you could ruin your relationship with your son—our son," and she looked at Sam with love in her eyes. Julia looked at Sam, too, and she could see that he was crying.

"Why did you have to leave us, Mira?" he asked.

She smiled and said, "But I haven't left you, Sam. See, here I am."

"Yes," he said slowly, "but it isn't the same."

"It doesn't seem to be the same because you are looking only at the impermanent. Learn to focus on the eternal—as Gabriel and Julia are learning to do—and you will realize that nothing ever really changes."

"How can I do that?" Sam asked.

"There are ways," she replied. "Listen to the young people. Learn from the tree and from all the spirits of the forest. This world is a place of deep learning, which often means forgetting the eternal in order to experience the lower levels of consciousness. But you experience them only so that you can learn how to transcend them. So now you must learn to listen, Sam. And, if you listen long enough, you will hear my voice again. I won't leave you until you're ready." With these words, the image began to fade until there was nothing left but a slight shimmer in the air around the tree.

Sam turned and looked at Gabriel and then at Julia and her parents. "Am I dreaming?" he asked.

Mother said, "I think we've all been dreaming and we're just starting to wake up." Then she reached out her arms to Julia and hugged her hard. "Let's start over," she said softly. Julia nodded and hugged her back.

Then Julia looked at Sam as he said, "Gabriel, come here, son." Gabriel slowly stood up and walked toward his father. Sam put his hand on Gabriel's shoulder and said, "I'm sorry I didn't believe you. I guess I just had to be shown."

Gabriel smiled and said, "That's understandable." He and Sam embraced, and Julia felt the whole forest glowing with the light that Gabriel's mother had brought and somehow left with them.

Father said, "I think we have something to celebrate. Let's forget about school and work for the rest of the day and go back to the cabin and have a cup of tea." Everyone smiled and said OK. Then he slowly walked up to the old maple tree. He put his hand on the trunk and gazed up at the branches. "Well," he said, "I don't know if you'll ever talk to me, but I have a feeling that none of us will be the same after this day."

17.

The Hunters' Club

Gabriel and Sam stayed for dinner that evening, and then everyone sat around the kitchen table and talked. Sam and Julia's parents wanted to know all about the conversations with the tree and Julia's experiences with the bird and the squirrel. And, of course, Sam, in particular, wanted to hear every detail concerning Gabriel's mother. Father said, "What did you say her name was—is?"

"Mira," Sam replied, "Mira, the beautiful one."

"She is beautiful," Father agreed.

"I've tried to put her out of my mind," Sam said. "I guess it just hurt too much to think about her. It's really a shift in consciousness to realize that she's still around."

"There's something I don't understand, though," Mother said. "I studied eastern religious philosophy at university and I thought that it was only the less advanced souls that stayed connected to the earth and the people they knew—because of their attachment, you know. But your wife—Mira—is clearly very evolved. Shouldn't her soul have moved on to the higher realms?"

"It's because of us," Gabriel said. "She isn't staying around because she needs us. It's because we still need her. She can come and go as she pleases."

"How do you know?" Sam asked.

"Because she told me. She said that there are lines of love that connect people and souls make agreements before they incarnate. These agreements can't be broken after that because love is eternal and unchanging. If one soul is more evolved, it has a responsibility to help the ones who aren't as advanced. She said that these lines of love really connect us with all people, but they shine brighter and exert more of a magnetic pull with the people we've made agreements with."

"So that's what the tree meant when he said that agreements are made beforehand," Julia exclaimed.

"When did he say that?" Mother asked.

"When he told me that Gabriel was my brother."

"Gabriel's your brother?" Sam looked amazed.

"Yes—I forgot to mention that," Julia answered. "He didn't mean biologically, of course—at least not in this lifetime."

"Amazing," Father said. "Well, you do relate like brother and sister."

Sam and Gabriel finally left around ten. Mother and Father hugged Julia and went to bed. Julia was tired, but she lingered in the kitchen. She was happier than she'd been in a long time. She had never felt so close to her parents. She still had some unanswered questions, however. She hadn't forgotten that the tree had told her to remember the seeds. She wanted to know what he meant.

She sat down in the rocker and started picturing various kinds of seeds in her mind—fat white squash seeds, tiny black carrot seeds, rough brown beet seeds, wrinkled pale green peas, shiny speckled beans—but what did he want her to remember about them?

Julia thought about planting the seeds last spring. She had poked little holes with her finger for the peas and beans and squash while Mother made rows with the hoe for the carrots and beets. Then Julia had held her hand over the rows and let the seeds slip between her fingers. Mother had come along behind her to cover them up and water them.

Julia pictured the seeds under the dark earth as the water seeped down and made them wet. She tried to imagine the outside of the seeds growing soft and the tiny sprouts starting to push up through the earth to find the sunshine. But what was this supposed to teach her? Julia yawned and got up to go to bed.

Two days later, Jim called and said that the meeting with the hunters' club had been set for the following Saturday afternoon. He said that Julia and Gabriel's parents were welcome to come and that he and Stella were inviting everyone to return to their home for dinner. Mother accepted the invitation and said she would pass the message on to Sam. Then Jim said that if anyone had anything to say to the hunters, this would be the perfect opportunity.

At lunchtime, when Father came in, they talked about the meeting and what they might tell the hunters. Mother said, "I'm sure that they won't all decide to give up hunting just because Jim has, but maybe we could at least ask them to respect the boundaries of the property and leave it as a refuge for wildlife as Dr. LaTendresse intends it to be."

"That's a good idea," Father replied. "Do you want to do the talking?" he asked. "I think you're better at that sort of thing than I am."

"I don't mind."

"Great, and how about you two?" Father added, looking at Julia and Gabriel. "Do you want to say something, too?"

"I don't know," Julia answered. "What do you think, Gabriel?"

"I don't know, either. Let's think about it."

"OK," Julia said. Then she turned to her father and said, "Well, Father, how about that music lesson?"

"Right after the dishes are done," he replied.

So that afternoon, they sat by the window and played music. Gabriel was learning to play the flute. His mother had been an accomplished flutist and he now had her instrument. He seemed to have inherited her talent as well because he was catching on fast. Julia could already play the guitar reasonably well. She and Gabriel were learning some of the duets that her parents played.

It was a beautiful afternoon. At one point, Julia looked out of the window and saw the cold November wind blowing the clouds past the sun. It seemed to her that the branches of the trees were dancing in time to the music. She felt her heart dance in response, and at that moment, the sun emerged from behind the racing clouds and the woods were bathed in light. Julia's fingers moved effortlessly over the guitar strings and, as she gazed out the window, she could almost hear all the voices of the forest raised in a joyful song of praise and thanksgiving.

The next Saturday, Julia woke up to a light snow falling from a heavy grey sky. She got out of bed, wondering what she could say to the members of the hunters' club that could possibly make a difference. After she finished the breakfast dishes, she decided to visit the tree. As she put on her heavy jacket, Mother asked her where she was going. Julia started to say, "Oh, just for a walk," and then she remembered that she no longer had to pretend with her parents. She smiled and said, "I'm going to go ask the tree what we should say to the hunters' club."

Mother smiled also and said, "OK." Then she paused as if a sudden thought had come to her. "Could I go with you? I have to talk to them, too."

"Of course," Julia replied.

Mother put on her jacket and they started down the path. As they walked, Julia explained the procedure for communicating

with the tree. "You have to close your eyes and make your mind still. Then you ask your questions silently and listen for the answer."

"I'll try," Mother said.

As they walked up to the tree, Julia looked at his bare branches. She put her hand on his trunk and closed her eyes. Mother did the same. Julia focused her mind and then said silently, "I've brought my mother, Irene."

They waited quietly for a moment and Julia could feel the wind blow the light flakes of snow against her face. Finally, she felt the vibrations of the voice of the tree as he said, "Welcome, Irene—what would you like to ask?"

Julia felt her mother's excitement and knew that she had heard the tree. Then she became aware of Mother's silent question—"We want to know what to say to the hunters' club. We want to know if we can make a difference."

The tree answered, "A loving thought always makes a difference."

"A loving thought?" Mother was surprised. "We're supposed to approach the hunters with love? But they've been killing the deer."

"They are your brothers and sisters and they can't hear you if you don't speak with love. Don't worry so much about what you're going to say. The Presence will be with you if you go with a pure heart."

"What is the Presence?" asked Julia.

"You will know when you feel it."

"Is it like Brahman?" she persisted.

"It is His gift," replied the tree.

Julia and her mother waited a few more moments, but all they heard was the wind blowing down from the hills at the back of the property.

As they walked to the cabin, Mother said, "I don't think I completely believed it until now. But I heard him—and we both received the same message."

"Yes," Julia said. "We have to approach the hunters with love and the Presence will be with us."

That afternoon, right after lunch, Julia and her parents got in the jeep and drove to the hunters' lodge, which was at the edge of the forest. Jim and Stevie were already there. Sam and Gabriel drove up a few minutes later. They all greeted each other and stood together in the parking lot. Julia was glad to see Stevie up and walking around. She realized that he was taller than she had expected. She could see the edge of his bandage peeking out from behind the collar of his shirt, but his arm was swinging free and didn't seem to bother him.

Jim said, "I will open the meeting and make my announcement. Then I'll turn it over to any of you who want to say something."

Mother said, "I guess I would like to speak briefly and I think Julia may want to, also."

Julia nodded, but she felt nervous and had no idea what she wanted to say. She remembered what the tree had said about the Presence and tried to calm her mind. She saw Gabriel looking at her. She smiled and shrugged her shoulders.

While they were standing and talking, Julia could see other people—mostly men—drive up and go into the lodge. Finally, it seemed that no one else was going to arrive and Jim said, "I guess we'd better go in." Together they all left the parking lot and walked up to the lodge.

The main part of the lodge was like a large living room. There were sofas and easy chairs and in the middle of the room, someone had put up some folding chairs. At one end of the room was a big fireplace with a raised hearth. A couple of folding chairs were set up on the hearth and several more on the floor at either side. Jim picked up a third chair and indicated that Julia and her mother should sit on either side of him. The rest of their group found places near the hearth. The people in the room had been laughing and talking together, but as Jim sat down and faced them, everyone grew quiet.

Jim cleared his throat and pushed his glasses back on his nose. "Good afternoon," he said. "As you can see, I've brought some friends with me." He gestured toward Mother and said, "This is Irene Stanley. She and her husband Jack are the caretakers for the property which borders this one. On my left here is their daughter, Julia. And over there beside Jack are Sam Jacobsen and his son Gabriel. Sam is in charge of the camp ground on that property." Then he turned his head toward Stevie, whose chair was just below and to the left of Julia's. "And, of course, you all know my nephew, Stevie, who I am thankful is able to be here with us today."

Jim paused and the hunters all clapped and cheered for Stevie, who blushed and lowered his head. Then Jim cleared his throat again and said, "It won't take long to say what I have to tell you. As you know, I made a terrible error last week. I shot at a deer, who turned out to be just a fawn, and I accidentally hit my nephew. The fawn was inside the fence of the neighbouring property and should have been safe, but he was killed. The Stanleys have been kind enough not to press charges, even though the fawn had been raised as a pet by their daughter, Julia, and her friend, Gabriel. For this I am eternally grateful and I can't ever really repay them. There is something I can do,

however. Because of this experience, I have decided to give up hunting and I am hereby announcing my resignation from the hunters' club. That doesn't mean that I'm turning against you as people. Many of you are good friends of mine and I hope you will continue to be. I can't, of course, expect you to make the same decision I've made, but I can urge you to be careful and to always respect the law—and to pay attention to all No Hunting signs."

Jim paused again. His audience was quiet. Then one man asked, "Are you sure about this, Jim?"

Jim said, "Yes, I'm sure." Then he added, "I think that Irene would like to say something to you."

Julia looked at Mother and saw that her cheeks were slightly flushed. She took a deep breath and began, "As Jim told you, it's our job—my husband's and mine—to protect the property we live on. This includes protecting the wild animals, who have taken refuge there. I'm sure that most of you do respect the boundaries and the No Hunting signs, but some people have not. The fence wires, which were just repaired this year, have already been cut once, and deer have been killed. As Jim said, we can't expect you to give up hunting, but we do ask for your cooperation."

Then the same man who had spoken before raised his hand and asked, "Do you folks eat meat?"

Mother shook her head and said, "No, actually, we do not."

Then the man said, "Do you disapprove of hunting?"

Mother said, "From living so long in the forest, I've come to appreciate all forms of life. Rather than saying that I disapprove of hunting, I would say that it saddens me to see a beautiful animal shot down in the prime of life. I know that you would say that many deer will die anyway—from starvation or from the coyotes, who prey on them—and I know that's true. Death is a part of life—for animals as well as for people—but somehow a death that occurs as a part of the natural cycle is less disturbing."

Mother looked around the room. Then she said, "There was a time when humans were part of this natural cycle. They

lived close to the earth and they killed only what they needed
to survive. That is no longer the case. People have lost touch
with nature and no longer need to hunt to live. There are many
other choices. As my family can testify, it isn't even necessary to
eat meat in order to be healthy. I think that many people go to
the woods to hunt because they miss being connected to
nature. It isn't necessary to take a gun with you, however. You
could take a camera—or you could just go."

She paused and looked around as if waiting for a reaction,
but no one spoke. Then she said, "I think my daughter wants
to say a few words."

Julia took a deep breath, just as her mother had done. She
still had no idea what she was going to say, but she opened her
mouth to speak anyway and the words started to come. "I just
wanted to tell you about our fawn," she said. "We didn't really
raise him as a pet. We tried always to let him be wild and asso-
ciate with the other deer. But we did become close to him and
he always came back to visit us even after he got big enough to
stay in the woods by himself."

She looked over at Gabriel and saw that his eyes were
shiny. She wondered if he felt like crying. Then she said, "I've
always loved to look at the deer because they're so beautiful, but
this was the first time I was able to see one up close. Usually,
they're too afraid and they just run off. But Fawn wasn't afraid.
He let us pet him and he ate out of our hands. He was always
gentle and playful. He wasn't afraid of Stevie either, and that's
why he died. If he'd run off, he wouldn't have been shot."

She paused again and waited for the words to come to her.
Then she said, "Jim and my mom both told you that they
couldn't expect you to give up hunting and I suppose that's true.
But, as for me, well I'm not expecting, but I am asking. Please,
don't shoot the deer anymore—and, if you do find yourselves in
the woods with a gun and you see a deer, take the time to look
in his eyes. Then you'll see that he isn't so different from you.
He wants to live and be free just like you do."

She stopped abruptly and looked around at her audience.
Some of the people looked stubborn and defiant and others
looked uncomfortable. Very few would meet her gaze. Then

she looked at Stevie, who was smiling at her warmly and nodding his head in approval. Finally, she looked over at Jim, who said, "Thank you, Julia and Irene. Now I'm going to turn the meeting over to the vice-president, Bill Blakesly—Bill ..."

A man wearing a red plaid shirt got up and came to the front. "Thank you, Jim," he said. "And thank you all for speaking so honestly although I have to say I'm sorry about your decision to resign. Are you going to stick around for the rest of the meeting?"

"No, I don't think that would be appropriate. Anyway, my wife and sister are waiting for us back at the house. So you carry on—you're the president now, Bill. We'll be in touch." He stood up and looked around at his group, who all stood up as well and followed him to the door of the lodge.

18.

Seeds

After lunch, back at Jim and Stella's house, they all sat and talked about the meeting. "I don't think we convinced anyone," Mother said.

"No," Jim replied, "but I don't think that was the point."

"I don't either," Father said. "When you do something in order to convince someone else, it usually doesn't work anyway."

"I think what we did today was plant some seeds," Jim added.

"Seeds?" Julia said with sudden interest.

"Yes," Jim said. "Seeds—ideas, that is—that could germinate and grow some day."

"Hmm." Julia looked thoughtful.

"Why, Julia?" Mother said. "What are you thinking about?"

"I'm thinking about seeds. I've been thinking a lot about seeds lately."

"Why is that?" Father asked.

"Because the tree told me to remember the seeds, and I've been trying to figure out what he was talking about."

"What tree?" Stevie asked, looking puzzled.

"Oh, yes," Julia said, "we haven't told you about the tree."

"I just thought of something," Gabriel interrupted. "There's a story in *The Upanishads* about seeds."

"Really?" Julia sat up straighter and looked at him. "Where?"

"I don't remember exactly—toward the back, I think."

"That has to be it." Julia was suddenly excited. "The tree would know I was reading that book. There has to be a clue. I'll look the minute I get home."

As soon as Julia returned to the cabin, she got out *The Upanishads* and sat down at the kitchen table to look through the book. She started at the back and scanned every page, looking for the word "seed." Once she found it, but it was only a reference to seeds, not a whole story. Finally, however, in the section called "Chandogya," she found something that looked promising. "This must be it," she said to her parents, who were cutting up vegetables for dinner.

"What does it say?" Mother asked. "Read it out loud."

"OK, I think it starts here." She looked at the pages that came before and said, "It's about someone called Svetaketu, or however you pronounce it, and he's asking his father questions about the Self." She began to read:

'Please, sir, tell me more about this Self.'

'Be it so. Bring a fruit of that Nyagrodha tree.'

Julia stumbled over the word "Nyagrodha" and then continued.

'Here it is, sir.'

'Break it.'

'It is broken, sir.'

'What do you see?'

'Some seeds, extremely small, sir.'

'Break one of them.'

'It is broken, sir.'

'What do you see?'

'Nothing, sir.'

'The subtle essence you do not see, and in that is the whole of the Nyagrodha tree. Believe, my son, that that which is

the subtle essence—in that have all things their existence.
That is the truth. That is the Self. And that, Svetaketu,
THAT ART THOU.'

Julia considered what she had just read. Finally, she said, "Do
we have any seeds?"

"We haven't ordered the seeds for the garden yet. It's too
early," Father said.

"We have sesame seeds," Mother said.

"Where?" Julia got up and went to the cupboard.

"In that jar." Mother pointed to the second shelf.

Julia took down the jar and brought it to the table. She
sprinkled out a couple of seeds. "They're so tiny," she said.

"The seeds in the story were tiny, too," Mother reminded
her.

"Yes, but how can I cut them in two?"

"With your fingernail. Like this." Mother picked up one
tiny seed on the tip of her finger and split it in two with her
thumbnail. "Get the magnifying glass, Jack," she said.

Father handed Julia the magnifying glass and she held it
over the two halves of the sesame seed. "What do you see?"
he asked.

"Nothing, except the two halves of the seed. They seem to
be solid."

"Well," Mother said, "in the book it says that the essence
of the seed can't be seen. Just like the essence of a person can't
be seen."

"Or of Fawn," Julia added.

"Or of Fawn. Once that essence is gone, the body itself is
nothing."

"And, in *The Upanishads*, it says that essence can't die,"
Julia said. "And that's the part that is what we really are. Hey, I
just thought of something."

"What?" Father asked.

"The tree told me a long time ago that I needed to remember who I really am. That must be what he meant. Who I really am is that invisible part that can't be seen, and," she continued, "according to *The Upanishads*, that part can't die either."

"Right," Mother said. "So if it can't die, it could appear again in another body."

"Do you believe in reincarnation?" Father asked with surprise.

"I don't know," Mother said, "maybe. I mean birth is such an amazing miracle. Why shouldn't rebirth be possible?"

Julia gazed at the broken seed again and then put down the magnifying glass. "One thing I don't understand is how we could see Gabriel's mother if the essence that survives is invisible."

"That's a good question," Father said. "Maybe you'll have to ask your tree."

"Good idea," Julia said. "I'll go right now."

"Take your boots," Mother said. "The snow's coming down harder. And hurry—it's getting dark."

Julia walked as fast as she could down the path. The air was colder and the wind had picked up. A light dusting of snow covered the ground.

When she reached the tree, she went right to the point. "I found the story about the seeds in *The Upanishads*. I understand that the essence which doesn't die is invisible. But one thing I don't understand is how we could see Gabriel's mother. She certainly doesn't still have her body with her."

"No," the tree replied. "She doesn't have her body with her. But Gabriel has the memory of her body."

"You mean he could see her because he remembers what she looked like?"

The tree was silent so Julia continued. "But I didn't know what she looked like—well, except I did see her picture once. Maybe that was enough—but wait a minute, my parents hadn't even seen her picture and they saw her, too—right here, when Sam was going to cut you down."

The tree was still silent so Julia said, "How do you explain that?"

"It takes only one mind to have a vision," the tree finally said.

"Only one mind? In this case, Gabriel's, right?" The tree didn't answer. Julia stood there for a minute, waiting. Then she realized that it was getting dark so she walked quickly back to the cabin. She came into the kitchen and said, "That soup smells good."

"So, did you get a response?" Mother asked.

"Yes, more or less. He said it takes only one mind to have a vision. Since Gabriel knows what his mother looks like, I guess he was able to make the vision of her body appear and somehow, all the rest of us were able to see it."

"Does that mean it wasn't real?" Father asked.

Julia smiled. "I know what the tree would say to that. He'd say, 'That depends on what you think of as real.'"

Mother laughed. "You sound just like my philosophy professor." Then she added, "I don't think it matters what caused Mira to appear to us that day. What's important is what we learned and that, I know, is real."

"True enough," Father said. "Lessons of love are always real."

"Love," Julia said. "Love is invisible, too. And yet it's the most real thing in the world. Do you think that it could be related to this mysterious essence we've been talking about—what *The Upanishads* call the Self?"

Mother and Father both looked at Julia and finally, Mother said, "You know, Julia, I think you're beginning to understand something very important."

19.

Friends

The snow continued for the rest of the week and by Saturday, there were several inches on the ground. "This is a lot of snow for the end of November," Father said as he sat down to breakfast.

"Enough to go skiing," Julia said. "Gabriel's coming over later and we're going to cut our first ski trail."

Just then the phone rang. "That must be Gabriel now," Julia said as she jumped up to get the telephone. "Hi," she said.

"Julia?" The voice that answered was deeper than Gabriel's and Julia didn't recognize it at first.

"Yes?" she said.

"Hi, it's Stevie."

"Oh, Stevie. Hello, how are you?"

"Fine. I hope this isn't a bad time to call. You did say you always got up early."

"No, it's fine. We're just eating breakfast."

"Oh, I won't keep you then. I've just been thinking about your mysterious tree."

"Ah, yes—the tree."

"You said that it tells you things. And you also said you'd explain some time."

"I did say that, didn't I?" Julia thought for a moment and then said, "Are you busy this morning?"

"No, why?"

"Because Gabriel and I are going skiing up here in the woods. Maybe you could come, too. Then we could introduce you to the tree."

"Introduce me? That sounds interesting. OK, I'll see if my mom will drive me—or let me take the car."

"You have your license?" Julia was impressed.

"Just got it. But I don't get to use the car very often. Anyway, I'll get up there somehow—with my skis. Around ten?"

"Perfect," Julia said.

Gabriel arrived at nine-forty-five. "We have to wait for Stevie," Julia said. "He's going with us."

"Oh, how did that happen?"

"He called this morning. He's been thinking about the tree."

"Are you going to take him to meet the tree? Do you think that's wise?"

"I think it will be fine."

Stevie arrived with his mother a few minutes later. Mary came in to see Julia's parents, who asked her to join them for dinner when she came back to get Stevie. "Ask Jim and Stella, too," Mother said, "and I'll call Sam."

Julia and Gabriel and Stevie put on their skis and headed down the path. When they reached the road, Julia said, "OK, I have to explain about the tree before we go there." She told Stevie about how the tree had first spoken to her. "He sounded kind of like my grandfather. I mean, you can't really hear him with your ears, but he reminds me of my grandfather. The things he says have a moral to them—or maybe I should say, a lesson. He can be mysterious. A lot of times, he just gives us hints and then lets us figure things out ourselves—it can be frustrating now that I think about it, but that's the way he is. I don't know for sure if he'll talk to you, but so far, he's been agreeable every time I've brought someone to him."

"Who have you brought?" Stevie asked.

"Well, Gabriel—and my mom. That's all."

"Your mom? How did it happen that you brought her?"

"Well, that's a long story. We'll tell you that one another time. Let's go to the tree now."

As they approached the tree, Gabriel pointed and said, "That's the one—the big maple."

Stevie looked at the tree whose branches were covered with snow. "Does he really talk to you even in the winter? He seems so still—as though he were sleeping."

"I guess the spirit of the tree never really sleeps," Julia replied. She took off her skis and walked up to the tree. She put her hand on his trunk and waited while Gabriel and Stevie took off their skis. Then she said, "You have to make your mind still and close your eyes." She and Gabriel both closed their eyes, too. Julia stood silently for a moment and then directed her thoughts toward the tree. "I've brought someone else to see you. This is Stevie."

She was surprised when the tree answered immediately, "He's come home now."

"Come home?" She heard the question and wasn't sure whether it had come from her mind or Stevie's.

"Yes," the tree said to Stevie. "You've been wandering long enough. You must bring your family home also. That's why your life has continued. There are reasons, you know."

"You mean that's why I wasn't killed by the bullet?" This time Julia was sure the question had come from Stevie.

"Exactly," the tree responded.

"So how do I bring everyone home?" asked Stevie. "And where's home, anyway?"

"It isn't a case of where. And, as for how, just continue. You are on the path."

Julia could feel Stevie waiting for further instructions, but she knew that the tree was finished for the time being. She opened her eyes and looked at Stevie. His eyes were still shut tight and he had a determined look on his face. Then she looked at Gabriel. He had opened his eyes the same time she had. He smiled and said, "Stevie, he's done. He won't say anything more."

Stevie opened his eyes and blushed when he saw both Julia and Gabriel watching him. He said, "But I don't really understand everything he told me."

"It's always like that," Julia said. "Just wait a while. It will start to make sense."

"But do you understand what he meant when he said I'd come home?"

"Do you feel like you're at home right now?" Gabriel asked.

Stevie looked around at the trees with their bare branches, dark against the falling snow. Then he looked at Julia and Gabriel and he grinned, "Yes, I guess I do, as a matter of fact—more than I have for a long time. Most people would think that the things you two talk about are crazy, but for some reason, they make sense to me."

"So you see," Gabriel said, "there are reasons for everything. It's no accident that we found you that day in the woods."

"No, I suppose it wasn't," Stevie replied. "In a way, getting shot that day was the best thing that ever happened to me—except for Fawn, that is. I still feel bad that he had to die."

"Yes," Julia said. "I do, too—but I think that there's still more we have to learn about Fawn."

"Like what?" Stevie asked.

"I don't know yet. I just have a feeling. Come on—let's put on our skis and go make our trail." She picked up her skis and laid them down on the road. "I'll lead first. The snow isn't too deep so it won't be so hard."

They skied past the cabin and Julia led the way up into the woods. The road rose gradually as they approached the hills at the back of the property. The higher they went, the deeper the snow became. Julia was soon out of breath. "This is harder than I thought," she said finally. "Gabriel, you can lead for a while."

"I can take a turn, too," Stevie said.

"But you don't know where you're going," Julia replied.

"That's true."

"Come on," Gabriel said. "It isn't that much farther to the fence line."

When they reached the end of the road, they stopped and looked around. Julia pointed to the left. "With the leaves gone, we can see the top of the pyramid rock where we found you," she said to Stevie.

Stevie looked at the rock for some time. Finally he said, "The last thing I remember about that day is talking to Fawn." He turned to Julia and Gabriel. "You know, you two are lucky not to be going to school."

"Why?" Gabriel asked.

"Because it's getting really weird there. There's a lot of pressure to do things I'm not sure I want to do."

"Such as?" Julia asked.

"Well, such as smoking, for example. A lot of guys I used to be friends with have started smoking. And they try to get other kids to do it, too."

"Did you ever try it?" Gabriel asked.

"Once—I got so sick I couldn't stand it. Then they called me a sissy and a nerd."

"What's a nerd?" Julia asked.

"Well, kind of an intellectual, I guess."

"Are you an intellectual?"

"I like to read. Maybe that makes me a nerd."

"Good," Gabriel said. "We like to read, too. We can all be nerds together."

Stevie laughed. Then he said, "There's also a lot of conflict between the French and English kids. Their schools are right next to each other and they fight sometimes in the parking lot."

"What do they fight about?" Gabriel asked.

"Beats me. It's strange because the adults seem to get along fine."

"That's true," Gabriel said. "Both French and English people come to the camp and they have a good time together. Most of them are bilingual—to a point anyway—and they all manage to communicate."

"I know," Stevie said. "That's the way it's always been out here. It's the kids that are getting weird—more and more so every day."

"Well," Julia said, "you can just come here and spend time with us. Let those other kids be weird if they want to."

"I'd like that. Maybe the tree's right. Maybe I have come home."

When they went back to the cabin for lunch, Mother said, "Mary, Jim, Stella and Sam are all coming for dinner. We'll need help with the preparations."

"OK," Julia said. "We'd like to go for another ski after lunch so what time do you want us back?"

"Around three would be fine."

"OK," Julia said again. "Does anyone have a watch?"

"You know perfectly well I have my watch," Gabriel said. He looked at Stevie. "Julia refuses to wear a watch."

"Julia is a free spirit," Stevie said smiling.

"Well, she may be a free spirit, but she still asks me what time it is. One of these days, I'm going to fool you and not bring my watch," he said to Julia. "What will you do then?"

"I'll do what I did before I met you," she said with a grin. "I'll just use my intuition."

Thanks to Gabriel's watch, they were back at the cabin at three on the dot. They sat at the table and talked while they chopped vegetables for the salad and grated cheese for the lasagna. Then they cut up apples for pies. "Looks like we're having a feast," Stevie said.

Jim and Mary and Stella arrived at five-thirty and Sam came a few minutes later. They all sat down to dinner not long afterwards. Mother had put the extra leaf in the table and it took up almost all of the space in the kitchen. As

Father put the lasagna on the table, he said, "Maybe we should have a blessing."

Everyone was silent for a moment and then Gabriel said shyly, "I know one."

"Go ahead," Sam said.

They all bowed their heads and Gabriel said:

Filled full with Brahman are the things we see,
Filled full with Brahman are the things we see not,
From out of Brahman floweth all that is:
From Brahman all—yet is he still the same.
OM ... Shanti, Shanti, Shanti.

When they raised their heads, Mary said, "Where did that come from?"

"I know," Julia said. "It's at the beginning of *The Upanishads*, except in the book, it says 'OM ... peace, peace, peace.'"

"Shanti means peace," Gabriel said.

"OM—Shanti—that's what my yoga teacher says at the end of class," Mary said.

"You're taking yoga?" Mother asked.

"Yes, there's a little yoga center—not far from here. I just started a couple of months ago. It's nice—very relaxing."

"I go, too, sometimes," Stella said.

"I used to do yoga when I was younger," Mother said. "I shouldn't have stopped."

"We do a little meditation at the end of class and my teacher tells us to repeat the sound OM to ourselves while we meditate," Mary said. "She said it stands for the primordial sound of the universe, whatever that means."

"It means the sound vibrations that created the universe," Gabriel said. "My mother explained it to me," he added. "And that prayer is the one she always said before meals. You remember, don't you?" he said, looking at Sam.

"Yes, son, I do remember," Sam said softly.

"That reminds me," Julia said to Gabriel. "We were supposed to be practising our meditation. Have you been?"

"Not really," Gabriel said. "I kind of forgot."

"Me, too," Julia said. "Maybe we could all meditate tonight after dinner. That would be fun."

Father laughed. "I'm not sure meditation is supposed to be for fun, but I'm willing to give it a try if everyone else is."

So after the dinner dishes were washed and the leaf was taken out of the table, everyone sat down on the floor in a circle. Mary said, "Cross your legs, if you can."

"I'm not sure that's possible," Jim said.

"Here, sit on this cushion," Mother said, handing him the cushion from the rocking chair. "Just sit however you can—any way that's more or less comfortable."

"Right," Mary said. "Now close your eyes and breathe slowly. Pay attention to your breath and mentally say OM every time you breathe in and out."

Julia closed her eyes and started to say OM to herself. At first, it helped her to concentrate, but then she forgot about it as she focused her mind down to a single point, the way she did when she talked to the tree. She saw the tiny beam of light appear and she watched as it grew larger and began to fill her whole mind. As she floated with the light, she suddenly remembered Fawn. She had a sense of his gentle spirit, waiting somewhere, like a seed underground, waiting for the moment of germination and rebirth.

When she opened her eyes fifteen minutes later, she saw that everyone else was looking at her, waiting for her to finish meditating. She felt too peaceful and content to be embarrassed. She smiled and said, "Jim said we were planting seeds when we went to the Hunters' Club. Well, I think we've just planted another seed. I'm not sure when it's going to germinate, but I know that it's going to grow into a really beautiful flower."

20.

The Secret

The snow did not melt. In fact, there were two more big snow storms and by the second week of December, there was almost a foot of snow on the ground.

"Well, at least we'll have a white Christmas," Mother said one evening at dinner.

"Yes," Father replied, "but I have to admit I'm already getting tired of shovelling."

"I wish I could you help you," Mother said, "but my elbow is still sore from when I banged it against the stove last week."

"No, I don't want you shovelling," Father said. "You just take it easy."

"I could help," Julia said.

Father looked at her and said, "You know what, you've gotten bigger. Maybe you could shovel."

"I'm sure I could. Next snowstorm I'm going to help you."

"Well, you won't have long to wait," Father said, "because it's supposed to snow tonight."

"OK, then tomorrow morning before school, I'll at least do the path as far as the jeep."

When the sun came up the next morning, Julia saw several inches of new snow on the path. She finished breakfast and started to take the dishes to the sink. "I can do the dishes if you're going to shovel," Mother said.

Julia found she enjoyed the shovelling. The snow was soft and the sunlight made it sparkle in the cold air. She knew that Father would take the big tractor to clear the road, but the paths around the cabin were too narrow and had to be done by hand. She felt so much energy from the fresh air that she did more than she had planned, and she realized she'd have to hurry to go meet Gabriel.

Julia quickly went back to the cabin to get her ski boots. As she came in the door, she saw Mother and Father sitting close together at the table. They seemed to be having a discussion. She heard Father say, "Well, we'll wait a couple of days and …" He stopped talking when he saw Julia.

"What are you talking about?" she asked.

"Oh, nothing," Father said.

"You were talking," Julia said. "I heard you."

Mother smiled. "It's almost Christmas. You shouldn't ask too many questions."

"Oh, then it's a secret," Julia said, "a Christmas secret."

"Yes," Mother said, "a Christmas secret."

"OK, I won't ask. I have to go meet Gabriel now."

Julia made it only a third of the way down the path before she saw Gabriel coming. "Sorry I'm late," she called out. "I was helping shovel."

"That's good," Gabriel said as he skied up and waited for Julia to turn around. "I was going to shovel this morning, too, but Réjean showed up out of nowhere and started doing it.

When my dad went out to talk to him, he said, 'You don't have to pay me for this. I just felt like being in the woods today.'"

"What did Sam say?" Julia asked.

Gabriel laughed. "He said, 'That's OK. I'm sure the rich doctor can afford it.' It's Dr. LaTendresse who pays Réjean, not us," Gabriel added.

They skied single file until the path widened and then Julia waited for Gabriel to come up beside her so they could talk. "It's starting to feel like Christmas," she said. "All this snow— and my parents are planning a secret present for me."

"That's neat. Secrets are fun at Christmas."

"Yes, and guess what we're going to do today during school."

"What?"

"We're going to decorate the Christmas tree."

"Did you cut down a tree for the cabin?" Gabriel asked in surprise.

"No, you know we don't cut down live trees. This is the little pine out in front of the cabin. We decorate it every year with cranberries and popcorn and other things the birds can eat. Inside we just put a few lights and ornaments on the big umbrella plant in the corner."

"That's a good idea. Maybe we could do something like that at the camp."

When Julia and Gabriel reached the cabin, they went to put their skis in the little shed. As Julia closed the door, Gabriel said, "Hey, look at that."

"What?" Julia turned around and looked where he was pointing.

"It's Réjean. He's finishing your path now. He must have walked up here after he finished at the camp. I don't see his truck."

"My dad's just now plowing the road so he couldn't have gotten the truck through." Julia watched Réjean as he steadily pushed the snow to the side of the path. "Gabriel," she said, "do you think Réjean is lonely?"

"Lonely? Why?"

"Well, he never mentions having any family."

"He never mentions much of anything. You'd think if he were lonely, he'd talk more so people could get to know him."

"Maybe he's shy."

"Maybe—or maybe he's just weird."

Julia and Gabriel went inside the cabin and found Mother sitting at the table surrounded by bags of cranberries and popcorn. "Oh, good, you're here," she said. "Could you start popping the corn while I try to find the little feeders we made last year?"

"I think they're in the closet," Julia said.

Father came in the door just as Mother was dragging a chair over to the closet. "What are you doing?" he asked.

"I'm looking for the bird feeders. I think they're up on the shelf in this closet—in that box." She pointed to a box which was underneath two other boxes.

"Here, let me get it," Father said. "Remember your elbow."

"Oh, yes, my elbow." Mother sat down at the table. "You can bring down all those boxes, Jack. I think the other two have the lights and ornaments for the umbrella tree." Mother turned to Gabriel. "Did Julia tell you what we're doing today?"

"Yes, I want to do something like that at the camp."

"Good idea. I'm sure we'll have cranberries and popcorn left that you could use."

Father placed the three boxes on the floor beside the table. "I'm going to go back out now and help Réjean finish the path."

"He's done," Julia said, looking out the window. Réjean had stuck the shovel, handle up, in a snow bank, and she could see his red hat through the branches of the trees as he walked slowly down the road.

By lunchtime, the cranberries and popcorn had been strung and Gabriel said, "What else are we putting on the tree?"

"Well, last year we made these little feeders out of yogurt containers," Mother said as she pulled one out of the box. "We fill them with unshelled sunflower seeds. And then we have these little balls of suet that we bought at the pet store."

"What's suet?"

"It's solidified fat," Julia said. "It's pretty yucky, but the birds like it."

"They need fat in the winter," Mother said.

After lunch, they all went out to decorate the tree. When the strings of cranberries and popcorn were wrapped around the branches and the feeders and suet balls were hung, they stood back to admire their work.

"It needs a star on the top," Gabriel said.

"But it would have to be made out of something the birds could eat," Julia said.

"I know," Mother said, "we'll make cookies. We have a cookie cutter shaped like a star."

"But won't a cookie get all soggy from the snow?" Julia asked.

"Eventually, but that will only make it easier for the birds to eat," Father said, "and then you can just replace it."

So the rest of the afternoon was spent making cookies. Julia dumped half a bottle of yellow food colouring in the dough and the stars came out a nice golden colour. Before they were baked, Gabriel poked a hole in each one so it could be tied to the top of the tree. Then before he left to go back to the camp, he climbed up on the stepladder and hung the star.

"That's better," he said as he stepped down from the ladder. "This has been a great school day—and tomorrow I'd like to do the same thing at the camp. I'm going to ask my dad to go get some suet balls and sunflower seeds."

"And I'll bring the cranberries and popcorn—and some star cookies for the top," Julia said.

By the following week, all the Christmas decorations were finished and wrapped packages had begun to appear under the umbrella tree.

Tuesday morning, as Julia walked out the door to get her skis, Mother said, "Do you want us to drop you off at the camp, Julia? We're going into town."

"What for?" Julia asked.

"Oh, we have a few errands to do," Mother replied, as she looked at Father and smiled.

Julia remembered the secret Christmas present they'd talked about the week before and said, "OK, I'll call Gabriel and tell him he doesn't have to meet me halfway—but are you going to pick me up, too? Because if you aren't, I'll take my skis."

"That won't be necessary," Father said, "We can pick you up."

When Julia got to the camp, Sam and Gabriel were just finishing breakfast. She said, "I know I'm a little early. My parents left right after I talked to you. They're going to town today."

"That's OK," Sam said. "Would you like to join us in a cup of tea before you start your lessons?"

"Sure," Julia said and she sat down at the table.

After they finished their tea, Sam gave Julia and Gabriel some assignments to start with and said he'd be back in an hour to do a science experiment with them. As soon as he left, Julia said, "Do you remember that secret present I told you about last week?"

"The one your parents are planning for you?" Gabriel asked.

"Yes, I think they're getting it today in town."

"Do you have any idea what it is?"

"Not at all," Julia said. "Usually, I have a few clues, but not this time."

"That's good then. It will really be a surprise."

The rest of the day, Julia kept thinking about that knowing little smile her mother had given her father. When they arrived to pick her up at three, she asked them what they'd done in town—just to see what they would say.

"Oh—things," Father answered mysteriously, "errands and things."

"I see," Julia said.

On the way to the cabin, her parents chatted about the weather and what they were going to fix for dinner while Julia looked out the window of the jeep at the snowy woods. When they got to the cabin, Mother made a fire in the cook stove while Julia and Father carried groceries in from the jeep. Then they all cut up vegetables for dinner. When everything was simmering on the stove, they sat down at the table for a cup of tea.

Julia looked at her parents and they smiled at each other again—the same secretive little smile she'd seen that morning.

Then Mother looked at her and said, "We have something to tell you, Julia."

"What?" she asked.

"Well," Mother said, and then she looked at Father with a big, happy smile and said again, "Well—it seems that we're going to have a baby."

"A baby?" Julia exclaimed. "But aren't you too old?"

Father laughed and said, "Not really, we were pretty young when we had you."

"But why didn't you do it sooner?"

"We wanted to," Mother said, "but it just didn't work out. We'd given up hope."

"Well, I'll be," Julia said.

"Are you happy about it?" Mother asked a little anxiously.

"Happy? Of course, I'm happy. It's something I've dreamed about. I'm just amazed, that's all." Then she jumped up and said, "I've got to call Gabriel and tell him."

Julia went to the phone and dialed Gabriel's number. He answered on the first ring, as though he were expecting her call. She said, "Gabriel, guess what? We're going to have a little baby sister—or brother. I guess it could be a brother."

"A baby?" Gabriel said. "Is that the secret?"

"I guess so," Julia turned to her parents. "Is the baby my secret Christmas present?"

"Yes," Father said.

When Julia hung up the phone, she came and sat down at the table again. She looked at Mother and said, "Tell me something. Did you really bang your elbow on the stove?"

Mother laughed, "Well, I did, but it wasn't too bad. Your father didn't want me to do any heavy work because of the baby."

"That's what I thought—and why did you keep it a secret?"

"We wanted to be sure. We didn't want you to be disappointed if it was a false alarm."

"So Julia," Father said, "are you satisfied with your Christmas secret? Is it a good present?"

"The best ever," Julia said. She jumped up and gave both her parents a hug and said again, "The best ever."

21.

Waiting

Christmas night Julia and her parents and Gabriel and Sam all went down to Jim and Stella's for dinner. As they were clearing away the dishes, Mother said, "That was a great vegetarian casserole, Stella."

"Thanks. Mary and I are learning a lot of vegetarian recipes since neither Jim nor Stevie will eat meat anymore."

"I just lost my taste for it," Jim said.

"I don't really mind," Mary said. "I know it's healthier and anyway, I heard that the real yogis don't eat meat, either."

"Speaking of yoga," Jim said, "maybe we could have a little meditation tonight. I kind of liked it when we did it before and it seems like a good thing to do on Christmas night."

"Let's end the evening that way," Stella said, "after we do some other Christmasy things."

"OK," Jim said. "What's next on the agenda?"

"Well, Jack and Irene and Julia and Gabriel all brought musical instruments. I thought maybe we could sing some Christmas carols. Stevie can sing tenor and I can sing alto if the rest of you can sing the other parts."

"Julia and I can sing soprano," Mother said.

"I can probably fake a base line," Sam said.

"Great. Then after we sing, I was going to ask Jim to read the Christmas story from the Bible."

"I'd be honoured," Jim said, "and I'd love to listen to the rest of you sing. My voice is better for reading than singing."

So Mother and Julia got out their guitars and Father and Gabriel picked up their flutes. "Shall we start with 'Silent Night?'" Mother asked.

Julia noticed immediately that both Stella and Stevie had beautiful, strong voices. They harmonized well and the other voices and the instruments sounded good, too. Julia thought, "We should tape this. It's so beautiful."

They'd been singing for almost an hour when Father said, "That's it. I can't think of any more carols."

"You sound great," Jim said.

"There's just one more song I'd like to do," Julia said. "'Amazing Grace'—for Fawn."

"That would be nice," Mother said, as she started strumming her guitar. Stevie and Stella sang the first verse together. Mother, Julia and Sam joined in on the second verse, and the flutes soared above the voices. When they finished, everyone was silent. Then Jim opened the Bible to the Gospel of St. Luke and began reading the familiar words: "In those days, Cesar Augustus issued a decree that the whole world was to be taxed ..."

Julia closed her eyes and listened carefully to the story of Mary and Joseph and their trip to Bethlehem. She pictured the young woman, heavy with child, exhausted and uncomfortable, and the man, anxious to find shelter for his family. It must have been a difficult night.

When Jim read the last words, he put down the Bible and closed his eyes. Julia closed her eyes, too. She didn't need to repeat OM this time. Her mind was already silent from the singing and the story. Hearing about the infant Christ made her even more aware of the baby growing inside her mother's body. During the meditation, she felt a strong connection to this little person.

On the way back to the cabin that night, Julia said, "This has been a wonderful Christmas."

The baby was due the end of August, and it soon became the focus of everyone's attention. Mother decided she wanted to learn to knit and Stella said she'd be happy to teach her. Julia and Gabriel said they wanted to learn, too, so Stella came to the cabin the end of January for the first knitting lesson. Mother insisted that she stay for dinner since she wouldn't accept any money for the lessons, and Stevie, Mary, Jim and Sam all joined them. The cabin was crowded, but the air was filled with music and laughter so no one seemed to mind.

After that evening, Stella came every two weeks to give the knitting lessons, which were followed by a pot luck supper,

music and a few minutes of meditation at the end. After one of the meditations, Jim said, "I don't know if I'm doing this right, but it does feel good to just be quiet for a while."

In the months that followed, the cabin began to fill up with baby sweaters, blankets and booties. During the music classes with Father, Julia and Gabriel learned some lullabies and in carpentry class, they started building a cradle and a high-chair.

One afternoon in late February, Father said, "As soon as the snow melts, I'm going to build a little room onto the cabin for the baby. You two can help me."

"Oh, I'd love to do that," Julia cried.

"Did the rich doctor's agent say it was all right?" Gabriel asked.

Father laughed and said, "Yes, he did."

In the science class with Sam, they began studying the process of reproduction and growth—in all species from plants to humans. They sprouted seeds and watched fruit flies multiply under a microscope. In the spring they planned to observe the tadpoles as they slowly changed into frogs. They had a book which showed the development of the human embryo in the uterus, and they compared these pictures with the ultrasound photos that Julia's parents brought home from their visits to the doctor. Toward the end of March, Mother said to Julia and Gabriel, "The doctor says that next time we should be able to tell the sex of the baby from the ultrasound. Do you want to know what it is?"

"Yes," Gabriel said.

Julia said, "It's a girl. I already know that."

"How do you know?" Mother asked.

"Because I can feel her in my mind. I think I've known her for a long time."

Mother smiled. She no longer looked at Julia strangely when she said things like that. The next day she and Father went to the doctor. When they got the results of the ultrasound, they discovered that the baby was indeed a girl.

That evening at supper, Father said, "Well, now that we know it's a girl, what are we going to name her?"

"Can't we wait until we see her?" asked Julia.

"Yes, I suppose so," Father said. "What do you think, Irene?"

"I don't mind," she said. "I think Julia has some ideas about the name and I'm willing to wait until she's sure."

Julia just smiled and said, "You know me pretty well."

"I'm beginning to," Mother said.

Julia and Gabriel continued their studies of the reproductive process as winter slowly came to an end and the snow began to melt. They collected the tadpoles and put them in a large aquarium where they could watch them grow. Julia told Gabriel that she'd never felt so totally connected to the life cycle before.

"I know," Gabriel said. "It's like waking up to the creation of the world every morning. Each day there's something new."

Spring passed quickly and the sun became warmer. Mother started to be uncomfortable and couldn't work in the garden so Julia had to take her place. The seeds went into the ground and were watered and then the tiny green shoots began to appear. Julia weeded and watered and mulched and watched the plants grow just as the baby was growing. She could see the baby moving around sometimes when her mother was sitting still, and Julia began to think about what it would be like to have a little sister.

When she wasn't out in the garden, Julia worked on the new room with Father and Gabriel. Sometimes Stevie came up and helped as well. He was as excited about the baby as Julia and Gabriel were. Julia had told Stevie that Gabriel was her brother so this baby would be his little sister, too. "You are more my friend than my brother," she said, "but you can share the baby with us anyway."

"Thanks," Stevie said. "I'd like that."

As August approached, the waiting became more and more difficult. The baby's room was finished, and the cradle and high-chair were ready. Julia also helped Father build a new dresser, and Mother filled it with diapers and tiny clothes. Mother was very big now and found it awkward even to walk—although she forced herself to go down the path to the road every day just to get some exercise.

One morning in early August during breakfast, Father said, "The green beans and tomatoes are ready to be harvested."

"I guess we finished the baby's room just in time, didn't we?" Julia said.

"Well," Mother said, "I don't think I can pick vegetables, but I can certainly sit at the table and cut things up."

"I can pick," Julia said. So after she did the breakfast dishes, she went to the garden and started harvesting the green beans. The air was warm and hazy. As she knelt on the straw mulch beside the bean plants, she realized that she didn't really have her mind on her chores. She was doing everything these days with a kind of dreamy expectancy as though the passage of time had narrowed down to a single point, which was focused on the act of waiting—waiting for the baby.

22.

Réjean

They worked on the beans and tomatoes for three days, and the following morning, Father said, "Today we take a break from the garden."

"Maybe you could go shopping," Mother said. "We're out of a lot of things."

Father said, "OK, let's make a list."

"Here," Mother said, "I've already made it." She handed him the list she'd written on the back of an old envelope.

"All right," Father said. "I'll be back in a couple of hours." He looked at Mother with concern. "Are you sure you'll be all right?"

"Yes, yes, it's still nearly three weeks before my due date. Anyway, we need groceries."

"All right, if you're sure. In any case, you can always call Sam if you need anything."

"I'll be fine."

After Father left, Julia did the breakfast dishes and then sat down in the rocker to think about how she wanted to spend her day off from the garden. She looked out the window. The sun was already warm. "If I'm going for a walk, I should do it now before it gets too hot," she told herself, but she didn't move from the rocker.

Mother said, "I still feel tired. I didn't sleep very well. I think I'll lie down for a while."

"All right." Julia continued to look out the window and suddenly, she realized that she should stay with her mother at least until Father returned. "It's true," she told herself, "the due date is still three weeks away, but just in case." She went to her room and settled down on her bed to read.

She'd been reading for nearly an hour when she heard Mother get up and go into the bathroom. A few minutes later, she heard her say, "Oh, no."

Julia sat up and put down her book. She waited a moment and then walked to the bathroom door. "Mother?" she called.

Mother opened the door. She had a strange look on her face. "Oh, Julia," she said, "call Sam right away. My water's broken."

"Your what?"

"The sack of amniotic fluid that protects the baby. It's broken. That means labour could start any minute."

"But you're three weeks from your due date."

"Yes, but babies do come early. Jack was right. He shouldn't have left." Mother looked worried. "Quick, Julia. Call Sam."

Julia went to the phone and dialed Sam's number, but there was no answer. "He must be outside," she said.

"Do you think you could go find him?"

"Of course, but will you be all right alone?"

"Yes, yes—hurry—you've got to find someone to take me to the hospital."

Julia put on her shoes and ran out of the cabin and down to the path she and Gabriel had made to the camp. Her heart was pounding. What if the baby came while Mother was alone? She had to hurry. Everything was up to her.

She ran so fast she was completely out of breath when she reached the camp. She went straight to Sam's little house. His truck was there, but when she knocked, there was no answer. In fact, the whole campground was unusually quiet. Then Julia suddenly remembered that Sam had announced one of his nature walks for this morning. Everyone in the camp had probably gone. These walks were popular because Sam knew so much about the trees and animals of the forest.

"What am I going to do?" Julia thought. "If I call, would they hear me? I wonder which direction they went in." She stood in the middle of the campground, looking around wildly, trying to decide which way to go when suddenly, she heard the sound of hammering coming from the community center. Réjean—she could ask him. He had a truck. He was a little strange, but there was no choice. She ran to the center and threw open the door.

Réjean was standing on a ladder, putting up some moulding. He dropped his nail and turned to look at Julia as she burst through the door. "Julia, what is it ?"

"My mother—her labour's started early and my dad's gone to town."

Réjean put down his hammer. "Come, we'll go in my truck," he said calmly.

Réjean drove up the logging road without speaking. As they passed the old maple tree, Julia looked out the window of the truck and said silently, "Please, please, don't let us be too late."

When they reached the cabin, Julia ran inside with Réjean following close behind her. She went straight to her mother's bedroom and found her lying on the bed. She said, "Mother, quick, I've brought Réjean. Come, he'll take you to the hospital."

Mother took a deep breath and then gasped, "I can't move now. The contractions are too strong." She began taking quick, light breaths and Julia saw the contraction move across her abdomen.

Julia turned and looked at Réjean with fear in her eyes. "I don't know what to do," she said.

Réjean stood silently, gazing at Mother, for a moment. Then he shook his head and said softly, "Boil some water."

"What?" Julia said.

"Boil some water. Get a pair of scissors and put them in the pan to be sterilized. Then get some string. Do you have tongs?" he asked as he went into the bathroom and started washing his hands.

"Yes," Julia called from the kitchen as she pulled a big pan out from the cupboard.

"Then have them ready—beside the pan."

When Julia came back to the bedroom, Réjean was standing at the foot of the bed, his hand resting lightly on Mother's abdomen. "Now, get some clean towels and washcloths."

Julia ran to the closet and pulled out all the clean towels. "Is this enough?" she asked.

Réjean smiled. "Enough for several babies, I'd say." He put a couple of towels under Mother and laid the rest on the bed.

"The baby's crowning," he said. "I can see the head. Look, when the next contraction comes."

Julia watched carefully during the peak of the next contraction. "Oh," she cried, "is that the head? It looks weird. It's all wrinkled."

"That's because the scalp is still compressed. It will straighten out."

"Is that wet stuff hair?"

"Yes," Réjean said.

They waited as Mother breathed with the contractions. Each time, more of the baby's head appeared. "A couple more good pushes and she'll be out," Réjean said. "This is a fast labour."

Just then, Julia heard the cabin door open as Father came bursting into the kitchen. "What's happening?" he called as he put his packages down. "Why is Réjean's truck here?"

Julia went to the bedroom door. "Father, come quick," she said.

Father came to the door and said, "Oh, no, I knew I shouldn't have left." He walked quickly over to Mother and took her hand just as she gave another push. "One more," Réjean said.

Julia watched intently as Mother gave one last push and the baby's head popped out. Réjean carefully curled his finger under the baby's shoulder and pulled out first one arm and then the other, and suddenly he was holding the baby, who was covered with a wet cheese-like substance.

Julia held her breath as Réjean put his finger in the baby's mouth. He pulled out some mucous and then tapped her gently on the back. The baby opened her eyes as her skin started to turn pink. She looked straight at Julia and began to cry.

Réjean told Julia to get the string and scissors so he could tie off the cord and cut it. Then he asked for a warm, wet washcloth. Julia watched as he washed the baby and wrapped her in a clean towel. He handed her to Mother and waited to deliver the placenta.

"Oh, Jack," Mother said. "Look at her. She's beautiful. I'm so glad you made it in time."

"She's perfect," Father said. He knelt on the bed. He put a pillow behind Mother's head and looked down at the baby.

"Father," Julia said, "your cheeks are wet. Are you crying? I never saw you cry before."

Father looked up and wiped his eyes with his hand. He smiled at Julia. "Tears of joy, Julia—and gratitude." Then Father looked at Réjean. "This isn't the first baby you've delivered, Réjean."

"No," Réjean said softly. He picked up the used towels and said, "Where do you want these?"

"I'll take them," Julia said. She put the towels in the bathroom and then watched as Father dressed the baby. "She's so cute," Julia said. "Oh, look her eyes are open again." She bent down over the baby. "Hello, little sister." The baby made a little noise and looked up at Julia.

"She looks like she's trying to figure out where she is. It must be a shock getting pushed out into the world like that," Father said.

"Oh, look, Jack, she's nursing," Mother said. "She seems to be really healthy, doesn't she?" Mother held the baby close and smiled.

"She's so cute," Julia cried again. "Look, she's patting you with her little hand."

"Excuse me," Réjean said, "I don't want to interrupt, but you're going to need a birth certificate. I'll go into town and get one."

"Oh, yes, of course," Father said. "We'd appreciate that."

Julia watched as Réjean turned and walked quickly out the door. Then she looked at her parents and said, "Is Réjean a doctor?"

"I don't know, but he's certainly trained to deliver babies," Father answered.

"He seemed to be in a hurry to leave," Julia said.

"Yes, he did," Father replied.

Julia watched as the baby drifted back to sleep and then said, "I'm going to call Gabriel now. The nature walk should be over—and Stevie, too." She walked into the kitchen.

A few minutes later, she returned and said, "They all want to come see the baby this evening. Is that OK?"

"Of course," Mother said.

An hour later, Julia heard Réjean's truck drive up. She ran into her parents' room and said, "Réjean's back." Then she went to answer the door. "Did you get the birth certificate?" she asked him as he came in.

"Yes." Réjean went straight to the bedroom. "Do you have a scale?" he asked. "So we can weigh her."

"I'll get it," Julia said and went into the bathroom.

The baby was awake, but she didn't cry as Réjean placed her carefully on the scale. "Six and a half pounds," he said. "Not bad for three weeks early." He took out a pen and started filling in the birth certificate. "What's her name?" he asked.

"Well," Mother said, "we haven't decided yet. Fill out the rest of the form while we think about it."

Julia stood and watched as Réjean wrote Father and Mother's names on the birth certificate. He wrote down the date and place of birth and then paused as he came to the line for the attending physician. Julia waited, curious to see what he would write. Finally, he gave a little sigh and wrote with a firm hand, "Michel LaTendresse, M.D."

"But, Réjean," Julia exclaimed. "That's not your name."

"Well, I'm afraid it is, actually."

Julia took the birth certificate and handed it to Father. "Michel LaTendresse, M.D.," he read out loud. "Well, well. So Réjean, the handyman is actually the mysterious Dr. LaTendresse. But, why Réjean? Or, I guess I should call you Dr. LaTendresse."

"Please, at least you could call me Michel."

"All right, Michel—why the pretense?"

"It's a long story," Michel said, sitting down in a chair in the corner of the bedroom. Julia sat down on the edge of the bed. "You see, this cabin was built as a retreat for my wife and me. We spent only two summers here and then she died. I couldn't stand to come here without her so I decided to retire and travel for a while. I'd made some money on investments so I didn't really need to work anymore. I went to Europe and Asia. I was gone for five years, three of which I spent in India."

"India," Julia said. "That's where Gabriel's mother was born."

"Yes, I know," Michel said. "I stayed in a spiritual community there called an ashram. The swami who was head of the ashram taught me to do yoga and meditate. I also learned about carpentry and other construction skills. When I came back, I was a different person. I thought about this property and decided to build the campground as a retreat for people. Of course, I didn't have a swami like the ashram in India, but I figured if I made certain rules—like no alcohol or cigarettes, only vegetarian meals and no radios or TVs, the camp would attract quiet people who wanted to be in nature."

Réjean paused a moment and then continued, "I wanted to participate in the construction of the camp, but not as the boss—the rich doctor, who owned the property. That wasn't who I was anymore. So I became Réjean. I put my agent in charge of hiring someone to manage the camp and I also told him to find a family to live in the cabin and take care of the forest. When the camp was basically finished, I went back to India for a year. When I returned, I was curious to see how things

were going so I became Réjean again and got myself hired as a part-time handyman. And that's it."

"Well," Father said. "It's an interesting story. And," he continued, "we're certainly grateful to you for being willing to help us even though it meant sacrificing your disguise."

"A doctor has to respond to a medical need, and I'm thankful I was able to help," Michel said.

"So, what would you like for us to do?" Mother asked. "If you want to continue to be Réjean, we'll keep your secret. Won't we?" she said, looking at Father and Julia.

"Of course," Father said, and Julia nodded.

"No," Michel said. "That won't be necessary. I think Réjean has served his purpose. I'm ready to be myself again. But, if you don't mind, I'd like to keep coming here and doing odd jobs."

"If we don't mind," Father said. "Of course, we don't mind. You're welcome anytime. Even if this weren't your property, you'd be welcome."

"Good, then that's settled." Michel smiled and stood up. He picked up the birth certificate which Father had placed on the bed. "So one last detail," he said. "The baby's name."

"Yes," Father said as he took the baby from Mother's arms. "Sit down in the chair, Julia. It's time you held your little sister. Maybe you'll have an idea about her name."

Julia sat down and Father handed her the baby. She looked down at her sister. Her hair was soft and reddish brown. Her eyes were wide and dark grey-blue. She looked solemnly up at Julia. "I do have a suggestion," Julia said.

"What's that?" Father asked.

"I'd like to name her Fawn."

"I thought you might say that," Mother said. "Well, it's a pretty name for a girl, don't you think, Jack?"

Father nodded and said, "Fawn it is then."

Julia held the baby up to her shoulder and said softly in her ear, "Welcome to the family, Fawn. Welcome back."

23.

Moonlight

When Michel heard that people were coming over to see the baby, he said, "Well, I'd best be going then."

"No," Father said, "stay. If you want to be part of this little community, then you need to stay and greet people. Talk to them. Tell them who you are and why you were Réjean for so long."

Michel looked hesitant. Julia said, "Father's right, Michel. Then you won't be lonely anymore."

"Lonely?" Michel looked surprised. "So you thought I was lonely, did you?"

"Yes," Julia said. "I know you were."

"Well, you may be right. It's been so long since I felt close to anyone, I guess I started thinking that lonely was normal."

"Well, it isn't," Mother said. "You have friends now."

"But can you people really get past thinking of me as the rich owner of the property?"

"If you can get past it," Father said.

Michel smiled.

Mother said, "I think I'd like to take a nap now while the baby's sleeping so peacefully." She looked down at Fawn, who lay in her arms.

"Here," Father said, "I'll put her in her bassinet."

"No," Julia said, "Let me hold her again." The baby stirred as Julia picked her up and then went back to sleep.

"After I rest, I want to get up and go out to the rocking chair in the kitchen so I can receive people properly," Mother said.

"Are you strong enough?" Father asked.

"Yes, Jack, I'll be fine. Maybe the three of you could make some soup for tonight."

Michel stood up and said, "I'd love to make a soup. How about you, Julia?"

"OK. Let's see what Father got at the store." She walked into the kitchen, still carrying Fawn.

"I'll bring the bassinet into the kitchen," Father said. "I'm afraid you will have to put her down, Julia, if we're going to make soup."

"Ok, I will, but she's so cute and so soft. I like to hold her."

"You'll have lots of opportunities. In fact, I'm sure you'll be a big help in taking care of her."

Julia carefully laid Fawn in the bassinet and said, "Now, sleep well, little sister. You're going to have visitors later."

By six, the soup was simmering on the stove and Mother was sitting in the rocker, holding Fawn. A few minutes later, Sam and Gabriel arrived with a loaf of fresh bread. Sam looked surprised when he saw Michel. He said, "Réjean, how long have you been here?"

Michel looked at Julia, who said, "That's a long story. We'll tell you when everyone else gets here."

"They're here now," Gabriel said as a car turned into the parking area.

Jim and Stella came in with a big pot of spaghetti and Mary and Stevie had a salad and some ice cream. "Oh, good," Julia cried, "a celebration." She took Fawn from Mother and held her up so everyone could see her. The baby opened her eyes and looked up at Julia.

"Oh, isn't she beautiful," Mary cried.

"What's her name?" Stella asked.

"Fawn," Father said.

"Really?" Stevie said.

Gabriel looked at Julia. She smiled at him and nodded her head. Then he said, "Could I hold her?"

"Of course," Julia said. "She's your sister, too. Here, take this chair."

Gabriel sat down and Julia handed him the baby. Fawn whimpered a little, and then her eyes slowly closed and she went back to sleep. "Fawn," Gabriel said softly. He stroked the baby's arm with his forefinger.

"Here, Julia," Father said, "help me put the leaf in the table."

"I can set the table," Mary said as she went to the cupboard to get the plates.

Sam said, "Before we eat, I want to hear the long story about Réjean."

Everyone turned to look at Michel, who was sitting quietly in the corner. "Could you tell them, Julia?" he asked.

"All right—well, you see, Réjean's name isn't really Réjean at all. It's Michel." Julia paused dramatically and then said, "Michel LaTendresse, M.D."

"What?" Sam cried, "but how can that be?"

"And that's not all," Julia continued. "Michel is the one who delivered Fawn. That's how we found out." Then she proceeded to tell the story of Fawn's birth. "Now, Michel," she said firmly, "you have to tell them why you pretended to be Réjean."

"All right." Michel cleared his throat. He briefly told the story of his stay in India after the death of his wife and how he'd felt when he returned. "I just didn't want to be known as the rich doctor anymore," he said.

"Oh, no," Sam's face turned red. "I remember I used that very expression—the rich doctor—the day you came and shovelled."

Michel smiled. "Yes, you see my point. But that's not who I am anymore. I mean I am still a doctor and I still have the money, but it's not what I identify with anymore. Do you understand what I mean?"

"I do," Julia said. "It's like the seed."

"The seed?" Michel said.

"Yes, in *The Upanishads*. The inside of the seed, which is invisible is the real Self. It doesn't have anything to do with rich or poor or doctor or handyman or any of those things."

"You've been reading *The Upanishads*?" Michel looked impressed.

"Yes, Gabriel's mother gave the book to him and he loaned it to me."

"I'd love to talk to you about it sometime," he said.

"That would be easy to arrange," Mother said. "Perhaps we could have a little discussion group on the book. I'd like that."

"Me, too," Julia cried. "Could we start tomorrow?"

"I don't see why not," Michel said, "unless it's too much for you with the baby," he added, looking at Mother.

"No, it's not too much. I'd enjoy it. I won't be able to do anything outside for a while and the baby's going to sleep a lot for the first few weeks so this would be the perfect time."

Julia looked at Gabriel and smiled. Then Father said, "Well, shall we eat now?"

After dinner and cleanup, everyone took a turn holding Fawn, who woke up briefly a few times. Then Julia lit the candle on the table and turned out the lights. She said to Michel, "We always end the evening with meditation. I think you'll like that."

"Yes, I will," Michel said. He sat down on the floor and crossed his legs.

"Hmm, I wish I were as limber as you are," Jim said.

"Yoga," Michel replied.

"See, I told you, Jim," Stella said. "You should come to yoga with Mary and me."

Jim laughed as he sat down on one of the kitchen chairs. "Isn't it a little late?" he asked. "After all, I'm fifty-five years old now."

"It's never too late," Michel said. "I was past fifty when I started."

"Really?" Jim said. "Well, I'll think about it."

After the meditation, Gabriel stood up and stretched. He looked out the window. "Look at the moon," he said. Julia went to the window. The forest was bathed in moonlight. "It's so bright you could walk without a flashlight," Gabriel said. He turned to Sam. "I'd like to walk home along the logging road, may I?"

Sam looked outside. "Well, it is bright, but I don't know."

"I could walk with him," Michel said.

"But your truck," Sam said.

"I could sleep on the couch in the community center and come get it tomorrow. I'm coming back anyway to talk about *The Upanishads*."

"Please," Gabriel said, looking at Sam.

"Well, all right, but Michel won't sleep in the community center." He turned to look at Michel. "You'll sleep on our couch. It's more comfortable—and more quiet."

"Thank you," Michel said.

"I'd like to walk a bit with them," Julia said.

"All right," Father said, "you can go as far as the old maple tree."

"Do you all have the dishes you brought?" Mother asked with a yawn.

"Yes, we have everything," Mary said. "Come on, Stevie—Jim—let's go so Irene can rest. This has been a big day for her."

Julia and Gabriel and Michel let Sam's truck and Mary's car leave first and then they started walking silently down the moonlit path to the logging road. Julia looked at the light shining on the leaves of the trees. The air was completely still and the forest looked like a fairyland. They turned slowly onto the road and walked until they came to the old maple.

"Let's stop here a minute," Julia said. She walked over and put her hand on the tree. She looked up at the moon shining through his branches. Then she turned to Michel, who was standing behind her. "You said he was an old soul," she said.

"Yes, I remember."

"Did he ever talk to you?" she asked.

"My wife and I used to sit here and listen to the wind blowing through his branches. We always said we felt a presence, but no direct communication."

"Well, come here," she said. "Put your hand on his trunk and close your eyes. Make your mind quiet and listen."

Michel did as she said and Gabriel came and stood beside him. Julia closed her eyes, too. The air was so still she could hear the slightest movement in the underbrush. She waited a moment and then directed her thoughts toward the tree. "Do you remember Michel?" she asked silently.

The words of the tree came slowly. "It isn't a case of remembering."

"What is it then?" The question came from Michel.

"It's knowing. If you know your Self, then you know us as well."

"Who's us?" Gabriel asked.

"Language is so limited," the tree replied. "There is spirit—that's all. Your mother, Julia's grandfather, Michel's wife, the little fawn—and many more are all present in the voice you hear in your mind." The tree was silent a moment and then added, "The voice of love."

They stood still in the moonlight for a while and then finally opened their eyes. Julia thought she saw a tear glisten on Michel's cheek, but she wasn't sure. He smiled gently and said, "Thank you. Now I understand."

"Yes, I think I do, too," Julia said. "I have to go back now so my parents won't worry. I'll see you tomorrow."

Michel and Gabriel started walking down the road toward the camp. Julia stood and looked up at the tree again. Then she closed her eyes for a moment, but there was nothing more she needed to ask him. She opened her eyes and started slowly up the logging road, heading back to the cabin.

 **AGMV** Marquis

MEMBRE DE SCABRINI MEDIA

Québec, Canada
2003